BERSERKER

KITTY THOMAS

BERSERKER

KITTY THOMAS

Burlesque Press

1

CHLOE

You hear people say all the time that they're afraid of flying. I'm not afraid of flying. I'm afraid of suddenly not flying. I'm on a business class international flight to Paris to study art—I know, what a cliché, right? I'm in an aisle seat right next to the emergency exit. This is the first time I've flown over water, and I have to say, I'm not loving it. I'm worried this could turn into an unexpected cruise at any moment, and I don't trust all the other morons on the plane not to inflate their toilet-seat cover—I mean life vest—before getting off the aircraft. Then we're all trapped because you can't get out if you've already pulled the tag to inflate the damn thing.

The flight attendant who gave the safety talk was a real comedian. That's where I got the toilet seat cover thing—not my own material. I feel like I should at least be up front about that. I'm rarely witty when thinking about plunging to my death from 30,000 feet in the air.

I think they should get rid of that tag and make everybody inflate it with that red shoulder tube thing you blow into. At least then we wouldn't have to worry about dealing with the risks of a pre-inflater.

My gods, I wish I had wings like a normal valkyrie. And I bet you don't even know what a valkyrie is.

A lot of people don't know what we are anymore, and it's just as well because in the human world we mostly blend in to society. Or we really try to. People know about werewolves and vampires and witches and ghosts, but valkyries... unless you're really into Norse mythology, probably not. Werewolves and vampires come from a different dimension than valkyries, though. But for some reason we all like to party here.

We don't ever see each other except in this particular dimension. The earth plane is sort of a neutral ground we can all be in. And witches actually are already from this dimension. They're just humans who are a little more hooked up to magic and other dimensions than your average person—just a little more awake.

For those who do know about valkyries, we have this reputation of being these sort of badass warrior queens, all terrifying shrieks and lightning and flying through the air. Our job is basically to collect the fallen slain who we feel would be best to fight for Odin.

And then some valkyries kind of just hang out in the mead hall and sleep with all the warriors. It's a little bit of a party hall. I mean, Odin's a smart guy. He's not going to have all these slain warriors with all this pent-up testosterone and no ladies to enjoy. And before you get all offended, trust me, the valkyries engaging in this brothel behavior, do *not* mind. In fact, there's a waiting list, and I'm kind of kicking myself right now for not putting my name on it.

If I got on the list now it would still be centuries before I could even get into the hall. This is a high demand experience. Masculine and growly does not even begin to cover what these guys are.

But that's all stuff that happens in my world, not so much the human world—at least not anymore. It's been pretty quiet in this dimension for my kind the last thousand years or so. Humans used to feed a whole lot of energy our way when they were polytheists, but then they got all hung up on this one god who none of our gods even hung out with, and it's just been downhill from there.

Few humans believe in the old gods these days, and most men aren't exactly engaging in any epic battles right now. The most epic battle I witnessed this evening was a guy yelling at some poor girl for not letting him on his flight five minutes late. It was a different flight—obviously—or I wouldn't have gotten on the plane either.

Man, I'd love to be having *that* argument right now instead of sitting in this questionable aluminum construction flying over the ocean. Sorry, I got sidetracked, so valkyries... Even if we aren't all legends in our own minds or particularly magically powerful, we all have one special gift.

We can calm a berserker, which is really about the most useless magical skill one can have in current year. I doubt I'll run into a berserker any time soon, and if I do, I already know to run the other way. My mother—also a valkyrie, I know, what are the odds?—told me about a thousand times: don't get involved. Crazy doesn't begin to cover what these guys are. Berserkers are about as much the stuff of forgotten legend as valkyries are these days, so I doubt there are any on the human plane at all anymore which is just as well.

And yes I just said I'd be on the list to fuck the warriors but don't get ahead of yourself... warriors and berserkers are not the same. Berserkers are warriors but not all warriors are berserkers.

I've listened to the same paragraph on my vampire romance audiobook about thirty times now. I can't focus—and it's the hot part. I've listened to this dude tell this girl how he's going to drink her blood until she comes enough times to memorize it. Not at all how it works, by the way. They pretty much just drink you 'til you're dead. But it's become this thing in these types of books where somehow the magic of his bite engages her nether regions and results in orgasm, which somehow also makes her blood taste sweeter to him. I can't make this shit up.

And even though I know enough to know that's not how it is, these are my guilty pleasure books because it's hot, so hot that if it really worked that way I'm sure I'd go throw myself on the mercy of the first befanged man I encountered so we could engage in this sexy symbiotic relationship together. If *only* that was how it worked. I sometimes wish I could live in these delusions and believe in them, but almost no one in this dimension believes in magic anyway, so we're all equally suspending our disbelief for the fantasy I guess.

I keep having to push the button to go back thirty seconds because I can't stop thinking about water landings. Maybe I should have downloaded a book about how to survive a plane crash. I'm pretty sure I'd be able to pay attention to that.

I glance up to find some kind of altercation going on at the front of the plane about twenty rows up from me. There's a huge hulking beast of a man waving his arms about and shouting. I can't hear what he's saying because of the audiobook droning on. The sexy biting has commenced, but I'm watching something far more compelling.

The angry guy is hot. So when I say he's huge and hulking, I don't mean he's fat. I mean he's like probably six foot four and the ceiling of the plane is about an inch above his head. I mean he's very well-defined with tattoos that desperately cling to and wrap around his muscles, caressing each inch of flesh on display to me... Sorry. Where was I?

Yeah, he's not wearing a shirt. I'm not sure where that went, but it's not on him right now. He has blue eyes and long dark blonde hair and... I pull out the earbuds to hear what's gotten him so upset.

But he isn't speaking English. I have no idea what language he's speaking. No... wait. Yes I do. He's speaking Old Norse. No. No. No. No. NO! I shake my head in disbelief, willing this to not be happening. Right here, on this plane is the magical evil unicorn I hoped I'd never meet, a berserker. And there's nowhere for me to run.

I glance to the emergency exit and imagine myself just jumping out of the plane, even though I know that wouldn't end well for me. Come on, Odin, where's a plane crash when a girl needs one? Because I've seen berserker rage and destruction, and right now I'm hoping for a plane crash to stop this guy. And remember how terrified I was of *that* outcome two minutes ago? My odds right now are better with a plane crash. Half the people on this plane—or more—could survive a crash.

No one survives a berserker.

I also find myself wishing I'd listened when my mother tried to get me to study Old Norse. But it's a dead language! Nobody speaks it on this plane—except berserkers in a rage. I doubt he even knows the words he's saying. They just come, like the possession of the rage itself.

I learned French instead, which is also useful, assuming I survive the flight to Paris.

The flight attendant he's yelling at stumbles back, and the berserker is coming closer to my row as he pursues him. It's our comedian flight attendant, the guy that was making all the safety jokes.

Why did I pick an aisle seat? With each step, the berserker eats up the distance between us, and even though his focus isn't on me, my heart thunders in my chest as though it can beat fast enough to outrun him.

There are security people on this flight. I'm not sure if they're air marshals or some sort of private security provided by the airline to keep each flight secure, but they have no idea what they're up against. They can't take him down. He's too strong.

I can tell you what's going to happen next, and I'll be as accurate as the Oracle of Delphi. When this guy reaches full Hulk Smash, he's going to get physical. Once he gets a taste of blood, there will be no stopping him. Every single person on this plane will die. That is a one hundred percent certainty because berserkers in a rage don't stop until nothing is left breathing. There's no guilt or innocence. No one to be spared. No thinking or considering or judging. Only mindless destruction and rage. It's as impersonal and damning as a category five hurricane.

And I really never thought I would think this thought but, I'm the only thing that can stop him. Me: five foot five inches and a hundred and twenty pounds soaking wet. Good luck, passengers.

He's right next to me in the aisle now. He's so close that if I get out of this seat, I'll be standing right in front of him. His attention is still on the flight attendant as he continues to rant in Old Norse.

"Sir, sir, if you'll just calm down. I don't understand what you're saying. Does anybody know what language this man is speaking? Is there a translator on board?"

The flight attendant says this as though every plane carries several translators in all known languages. But the odds of an expert in Old Norse Studies being on this plane is even slimmer than the lucky-translator scenario. Then again, what are the odds of *me* being on this plane?

The security people or air marshals—or whatever they are—close in behind him. This is about to get physical. I have to act now before it's too late and people start dying.

I've never actually used my powers. I theoretically know how they work, but I was kept far away from these guys, so it's all theory. What if it doesn't work? What if he turns on me? Of course this is crazy thinking. He'll turn on me anyway if I don't stop him. I realize there are tears tracking down my cheeks, and I'm shivering like I'm lost out in a snow storm.

I take a deep breath, close my eyes, and lay my hand over his bare arm. Snake tattoos entwine under my fingers, and for a moment I'm sure they'll come to life and strike. The entire plane goes silent. Everything stops.

Some turbulence would be super great right now.

He says something to me, again in Old Norse, and now his anger moves in my direction. I can feel it, electric sizzle in the air. I rise on shaking legs out of my chair, leaving my right hand on his arm. I place my left hand over his heart and look up into his furious eyes.

"Just breathe, and put the beast back in the cage."

His eyes widen as I watch his body visibly relax out of the aggressive stance he was in. I can't stop trembling, the adrenaline is running too high. At the same time I'm so relieved it's working. He's calming down.

"What are you doing to me? What are you?" And he's back to English. Great, because I can't do this with a language barrier.

"Just breathe. Put the beast back in the cage," I say again.

He looks like he'll question me, as if he doesn't know how to do what I'm asking him to do. But the berserker inside him speaks my language—well maybe not my literal language—but it feels the energy. It knows, and it settles and fades into the background, leaving only the man behind.

"Ma'am do you know this man?" It's one of the security people.

We aren't supposed to be doing magic otherworldly things in front of normal humans. There are good reasons few humans believe in magic and those from the magic dimensions are all in agreement on this. Humans tend to run around murdering their own at the slightest whiff of magic. And we'd all just rather not get burned to death, thank you very much.

Luckily nothing extreme or obviously supernatural just happened. I mean there were no fireballs or anything. No demons whizzing about the plane cabin. Nobody disappearing or levitating. Nothing turned into a frog.

All anybody saw was a woman touch an angry man, say soothing words to him, and him calm down. That's sort of normal. Right?

"Ma'am?"

"N-no," I say, wondering if I should lie.

The berserker's eyes are locked on mine, and I can't seem to tear my gaze away or remove my hand from his chest. Finally I do pull my hand away because it's gotten very inappropriate and almost in the borderlands of sexy. When I do, I look down to see a black tattoo where my hand was pressed: Two ravens encircling an eye. Runes are worked into the design in a way that seems like a specific message instead of random decorative characters. Usually when it's just decorative, it's a circle of all the runes, sort of like: "Beyold ye olden viking alphabet!"

I didn't learn how to read runes either, so I don't know what the tattoo says. But these are all symbols of Odin. Maybe I was wrong and this guy *does* know what he is. He certainly seems to have pledged his allegiance to the king berserker himself.

He reaches out and cups the side of my throat like he's going to grip me and pull me into a passionate kiss or something. His eyes flash and glow golden then go back to electric blue so fast, anyone who saw it would think it was a trick of the light. Then he shakes himself out of whatever haze he was in and pulls away.

"Ma'am, I need you to step away from him. We're going to have to take him into custody."

I'm pretty sure if they try to take him into custody he's just going to go berserk again, and if I use this parlor trick twice in front of all these people they're going to know something isn't right. And even though it's a life-or-death situation and hundreds of lives are at stake—including my own—I don't want to play fast and loose with the rules. There are consequences to being showy with one's magic.

"Wait. I-I lied. I'm h-his sister. He has a condition." I really hope they don't ask me what condition makes a guy do something like this. Berserker Rage is not in any handbook or diagnostic manual that I'm aware of.

"We still need to take him into custody."

I round on the security guy, buzzing a bit from the berserker's rage and my close exposure to it. "And where are you going to take him into custody on a fucking airplane? You going to fingerprint and book him up here, too?"

The security guard actually takes a step back, which is hilarious because he's only feeling the residue of the berserker's energy, and he didn't seem too troubled when it was coming out of the guy himself. Maybe it's more jarring coming off me. I look too sweet and innocent for this kind of rage.

"Look, he's calm now. We weren't able to get our seats together, and he's agitated, so if someone could trade seats so we can sit together..." I trail off.

The person who was sitting beside him farther back on the plane jumps up to switch seats with me. He isn't keen on the prospect of sitting next to this guy for even one more minute.

Another flight attendant comes up holding a shirt in his hand. "Sir... we have a shirt and shoes policy on this plane. I'm afraid you'll need to put this shirt back on."

I'm so annoyed right now. I'm still trying to diffuse this energy safely out into the air, and none of these dimwits have any idea what I'm doing or the level of concentration it requires.

"Or what? In case you haven't noticed we're over the ocean. Are you going to kick him off the plane? And isn't it about time for food? We were promised an in-flight meal. It feels like food time to me. So why don't you all toddle on back to the area where the food is, do your jobs, and stop worrying about my brother's fashion choices."

At this point I'm far more enraged than he is, because energy doesn't exactly just disappear. It's not *my* berserker so it's not a thing living inside me, but it's still pretty intense. I'm probably the only person in the world who can claim supernatural energy interference for my current bitchy attitude. Except I can't because of the secrecy rule. And no one would believe it anyway. It sounds a bit too much like blaming PMS.

I take a deep breath and close my eyes, pushing the remaining dark restless energy out until I'm calm again. Then I go sit with this guy several rows back from mine. I don't want to sit with this guy. It's far too risky; too much could happen in the two hours we still have on this flight. But if I separate from him, the berserker could come back. And I can't risk doing that magic trick twice with this many witnesses. Even the stupidest human would figure out something unusual was going on. Probably.

I can sense he's young. I don't mean his human years, I mean the amount of time he's had the berserker with him. Valkyries are born. Berserkers are made. And I'm not sure how this one was made, but he feels new, like this may be his first full rage. I doubt he has any idea what the hell is happening to him, but as my mother says, "Not your monkeys, not your circus." And I swear, I'm not making this up, she stitched that saying on a pillow. There was a little monkey on it and everything.

"Umm, can I have the aisle seat, I don't like to feel trapped," I say to the man. As huge as he is, him being on the aisle would be even more disconcerting than usual. I'm still upset that my emergency exit is ten rows away from me.

"Sure." He slides into the seat the other man just vacated and I take his aisle seat.

"I'm Cade," he says, holding a hand out to me like we're business partners now.

I stare briefly at his hand, then put my earbuds back in and pretend I'm listening to my audiobook. But even if I could focus, I can't listen to my audiobook because this is still the sexy part, and I don't need to be thinking these kinds of thoughts next to the berserker. It's way too risky. Even just his proximity is... doing things to me. This is probably the most masculine man I've encountered in years. Yes, this dimension really is that sad now.

He taps me on the arm and I pull out one earbud. "What?"

"What did you do to me back there? What are you?"

"I don't know what you're talking about." This lie sounds dumb even to me, but I'm not about to get into a conversation about our origin stories with so many people so close by. And I don't want to bond in any way with this guy. Yes, he's hot, but he's a berserker and that's a big no for me. Hard pass. Nope. No, thank you.

The inedible cardboard they call food interrupts us and we eat, then I put the earbuds in, recline my chair the whole two inches I'm allowed, and pretend to sleep. He taps me on the arm a couple more times during the flight, but I don't break the ruse of my fake slumber.

When we land and are given the all-clear to disembark, I leap out of my new seat, race to my old seat, grab my bag, and get off the plane before most people have even managed to unbuckle their seat belts. They forget it's not a button you push like a car seat belt. Nobody listens to the safety talk.

I run through the terminal, grateful I didn't bring any luggage that had to be checked. I'm in Paris for a full glorious six months. I have a host family I'm supposed to be staying with, but they're on a trip and won't be back in the country for a few days so I've got a hotel booked until then.

I plan to buy whatever I need once I get settled in. I know the air marshals are arresting him, but he's unlikely to go for that. I don't know how much death and destruction will take place, but I can't be near him again. I won't sacrifice my life and freedom for a bunch of strangers. I don't care how selfish that sounds, I just won't do it. I'm not here to save the world from berserkers.

Thirty minutes later I'm locked safely in my hotel room. It's simple and clean. I order some room service because the plane food was so bad I think my body didn't even recognize it as food.

I wash my hands and my face and look up into the mirror to find my worst fear manifesting right before my eyes. The berserker marked me.

2

CADE

The girl is off the plane before I can say another word to her. I've never had a woman brush me off that hard. It kind of stings. I want to know who the fuck she is, *what* the fuck she is, and what the fuck she did to me. I've got a pounding headache, and I'm exhausted. I feel like I could sleep for about a year and still not feel properly rested.

"Remain in your seat, Mr. Wolf."

I feel the overwhelming urge to punch this asshole in the face. He just has that kind of face. But I stay where I am. I still don't know what I was so angry about or why I was yelling or what I was saying. I don't know the language that was coming out of my mouth, and that scares me more than the rest of the episode. Was it an episode? Did I have some kind of psychotic break?

I resist the urge to scratch at my newest tattoo. It itches more than normal, and it feels like the ink is trying to crawl out of my skin. I pat it a few times to try to settle the sensation without ruining the art. I'm vaguely familiar with the symbolism of the tattoo. There are runes, two ravens, and an eye.

The eye represents the eye Odin sacrificed for knowledge, and the ravens are his ravens. I don't know what the runes say, and the artist didn't tell me. But it looked cool in his design book, and more than one person has told me I look like a time traveling viking. So it seemed like an obvious choice for new ink.

When the rest of the passengers have disembarked, they put the cuffs on me and escort me off the plane. I'm not sure if one has the right to remain silent in France. I wonder if they'll deport me. I didn't have any world-shattering plans in this country—just a little break from life. I think normal people call them vacations. I'm fortunate I can take these breaks without anything in my life falling apart. This is what happens when you run a nearly fully automated online information product business.

I was a serious student of the Four Hour Workweek. And it's paid off.

I'm taken to a small room in what I'll call the airport security area... meaning not in view of travelers. I recognize the security people from the plane. They appear cautious of me, and I don't exactly blame them, even though my memory of what happened is beginning to fade. It was just a couple of hours ago, but I only have the vaguest recollection that I got into some sort of argument with a flight attendant about something and then there was that girl.

It's so strange. Even she is fading now, and only a few minutes ago she was so clear in my mind.

"Have a seat, Mr. Wolf."

The man in front of me has a grim look on his face and doesn't seem inclined to tell me his name or read me any version of Miranda rights. I don't even know if this is legal. He's French but speaks perfect, if heavily accented, English.

He attaches a second handcuff which is bolted to the table to my handcuffs, to ensure I don't get away somehow. There are about six armed men in the room so I'm not sure how they think *I'm* the threat right now. I'm not even armed.

"I'd like to speak to a lawyer. I'm an American, I know my rights." These words come out... not calmly, more... disoriented. It's as though I'm not familiar with my own language somehow. I find myself stumbling over words I've known and spoken since childhood.

He ignores my request, something I'm definitely sure is not okay or standard procedure. But I really only know what I've seen in movies, and even that's hazy at the moment. I've never had a reason to know what happens in these situations, but everything about this seems unreal somehow, like I'm having a dream and therefore nothing *needs* to make sense. If I just go along with it, I'll wake up at some point.

My head feels fuzzy again, like it's been stuffed full of cotton. The sound of his voice seems to alternately amplify and shrink in a dizzying sort of way.

"Did you hear me?" he asks, his voice low and gruff, sinister almost.

"I'm sorry, what?"

"Your sister. We'll need to question your sister."

"Who?"

"The girl!" he says impatiently.

"I don't have a sister." But all I can think is: What girl? Was there a girl? Does he mean a child or an adult woman? Was there a child in my care? What the fuck is happening to me?

"Could you tell me what language you were speaking on the plane?"

"I'm speaking English," I say, even more confused.

"What language were you speaking *on the plane*, Mr. Wolf, when you were shouting at the flight attendant."

"I-I don't know what you mean. I only speak English."

"This isn't working. Let me handle this my way." These words are spoken by another man, about my height. He's only bigger than me because he's out of shape. It's fat, not muscle. I could take him if I wasn't chained to a table and outnumbered by people with guns.

"Why am I here?" I ask. "I want to know why I'm being held. I didn't do anything wrong! I didn't do anything!"

I don't know what's happening. Why am I here? Why am I in handcuffs? Who are these people?

"I think we should call in a psychiatrist," the first man says.

"Nah, he's faking. Give me five minutes with the motherfucker, and he'll stop playing games with us." This is that second guy again. He slams his hand on the table right next to me.

I'm a big guy, and I don't startle easily, but I find myself jumping anyway at this obvious intimidation tactic. I'm so disoriented. Who the hell are these people?

"Why am I here?" I ask again.

"That's a convenient fucking memory you've got there." The second guy. "You shouted in another language at more than one of our flight attendants and made a very aggressive scene up in the air."

"No. That never happened. I wouldn't do something like that. I only speak English."

A recording device is placed on the table, and the first guy presses a button. I hear my own voice play back to me, only it sounds more guttural and somehow... inhuman. The words aren't English. He clicks the box off.

"Only speak English, huh?"

I stare blankly at the device. The second guy moves around behind me and grips the back of my neck surprisingly hard.

A loud growl rumbles in my chest. I think I'm having a psychotic break with reality because this sound isn't possible for a human to make. I sound almost like a wolf. But it isn't my imagination. They heard it too because they all take a jumpy step back.

My vision goes red. And I mean this literally. It's as though there's a red film in front of my eyes or like I'm wearing red-tinted glasses. The growl comes out of me again as I look around the room, meeting the eyes of each person until each man looks away, unnerved.

What am I doing in this room? Then the words come out of my mouth fast and fluid like water. Words I don't understand.

THE BERSERKER

(A ROUGH TRANSLATION FROM OLD NORSE)

Oh, look at these smug bastards—pissing themselves, but still somehow smug. They thought they'd gang up on one lone person, a stranger in a strange land. I growl louder at them, then I rip the cuffs apart, freeing my hands in one swift movement.

"Who are you to chain me, human?"

He speaks in a stupid language I don't understand and don't care to understand. I'm done talking.

Blood. Bones. Sinew. Guts. Organs. Glorious screams. Like the battlefield. They each plead for their life weakly, pathetically. Even in their foreign tongue, I know those words. They sound the same in every language. What have men become in this age? Shameful weakness. But all I see is the redness, the mad haze, the rage. I have always been angry, from my very first moment in every form I've taken. I am rage. I am fury. There is nothing else.

Except her.

I raise my mouth from the throat of the last guard, taking one last taste of the blood gurgling from his throat. He convulses for another moment then falls. They all lay around the white room, a contorted macabre display arranged for my viewing pleasure— taking the edge off my fury.

The rage fades the tiniest bit so I can think, the first pure clear thought I've ever thought. In this form, at least. Her. The girl. Blonde. Beautiful. Petite. And... *mine*.

I feel her in my veins. The memory of her warm hand on my chest. Like an angel saving me from myself. I am but a piece of a larger anger, and that piece, like every other piece, has a mate. A valkyrie. Some of us go centuries before we find her, and yet mine was here at my birth, my first expression in this world. I am only a day old, but at the same time I am immortal. Ageless. Timeless. Full of the knowledge of all the other parts of me and all the other lives they've lived. It's useful knowledge to have from one's first day. It makes the initiation into a new form much more smooth.

Not like humans who seem to have full-fledged memory wipes with every incarnation, like starting over on the game board and learning all the rules over again endlessly. That's a special kind of hell. I think I'd be driven mad if that's the way it was for us.

I laugh out loud. I'm already mad. No driving required.

I turn to see a mirrored wall. It's one of those two-way mirrors where other people can see in and watch. I wonder if anybody watched. Either they did and they're too scared to come inside or they're waiting for me with what they think is a plan. If they didn't catch the show, they'll know when they watch the video footage that I am not human. I move far too fast. They'll have to watch it in slow motion to see everything, and they won't want to see everything.

Most humans are far too sensitive for the gory details. They want artistic flashes and camera angles, not the stark slow pan of reality.

I take a look at my new form. It's nice. I appreciate that this human took the time to work out. I remove the destroyed bloody T-shirt, and take a good long look at myself. I wipe the blood from my mouth.

I smile and explore the different facial expressions this human can make. Soon I will know all that he knows and he will know all that I know as his soul merges and bonds together with mine. He doesn't know it yet, but he's no longer fully human. He's me, and I am him.

I touch the tattoo on his chest. My chest. Two ravens encircling an eye. And the runes... *Forever pledged to Odin.* Yes you are, my foolish friend. Perhaps you should have been more careful to understand the markings being permanently etched into your skin.

The only thing I want more than blood and death and destruction is her warm hand against my skin again. I could exist for a thousand lifetimes in that peaceful place, the only relief from the fury. It's only her influence that makes it possible for me to control the rage now. Yes, this display... this little massacre... that's control. But it won't last. I need to track her and get another hit of the good stuff before I truly lose it and very bad things start to happen. To others.

I wonder if she knows I marked her. I wonder if she's scared. Run little rabbit... Run far and fast. I enjoy the hunt.

3

CHLOE

I keep staring at my reflection, willing it to go away. The tears started several minutes ago, and I can't make them stop. I'm in mourning for my life and my freedom. Because those things are over now. There will be no studying art in Paris. There will be no seeing the sights. And I can never meet my host family. I can't risk their lives, too.

The berserker marked me. I sweep my trembling fingers over my throat; the skin burns where he touched me. It's not something a human would see. It's more like an aura—like a glowing golden energy that pulses from the place where his hand touched my neck ever so briefly. That single touch was all it took to tie my fate to his. Only another creature who is *other* would be able to see it.

And none of them will help me. They'll take one look at the mark and they'll flee like the cowards they are because no one stands between a berserker and his mate.

His mate.

Shit. I am in so much trouble right now. Technically I'm not his mate yet. I mean he *thinks* I'm his mate; he marked me after all. But it's not a complete claim—it's not finished yet. I shudder at the thought of what needs to happen for a claim to be completed.

I have one shot to save myself. If I can elude him for just a few weeks, his mark will fade, and he won't be able to find me.

I'm so tired. I just want to sleep, but I can't sleep here. And that's the real problem. Can I sleep anywhere? He'll be able to sense me, to track me. This mark is basically a GPS tracking device. There is no door, lock, or building strong enough to keep him out—no one strong enough to protect me.

A plane! I need to get on another plane. I can't believe I'm thinking this. Did I mention how much I hate flying? But I need to stay in the air, fly from place to place and sleep on the plane and wait this out. I'll be safe in the air. It'll likely drain every ounce of my savings, but I'll be safe. I take a deep breath and try to stop the trembling in my limbs from my all but shattered nerves.

I could try to go back to my world, but the problem with that is... there are a lot of berserkers in my world, and those berserkers? They're all kind of ... made of the same stuff. They have this strange hive-mind connection. They'll smell the mark, and they'll make sure I'm returned to my rightful mate. There's no safety there.

I grip the bathroom counter and stare myself in the eyes in the poorly lit mirror.

"Chloe. You can do this. You've got this. You are a valkyrie. Valkyries aren't afraid of anything."

This is actually true. Well, except me. I'm afraid of everything. It's like a vampire with a blood phobia. It's completely ridiculous. Maybe I'm not the only one. Maybe other valkyries are afraid, but we only hear about the ones who make a name for themselves. And they're all fearless badasses. So maybe it's a skewed sample. Maybe I'm somehow normal.

I can't fly out from Paris. He could still be there. He could be waiting for me. I turn on the TV, but there's no news of any death or mayhem. Maybe they aren't reporting it. But how could they hide such a thing? He would have killed everyone at the airport by now. That's a lot of people, impossible to cover up.

There hasn't been a berserker spotted in this dimension in so long there's no real protocol to deal with them. They aren't held to the same rules of magic secrecy because there's nothing they can do about their rages.

The only way to manage a berserker is to keep a valkyrie with him at all times to soothe and manage the beast. But I have my own life, my own ambitions. I don't exist to be some anger management therapist for one of these brutes, nor do I exist for the other purposes he'd keep me. Not that he isn't incredibly hot. On a certain level it's hard to be horrified by the idea of that body on top of mine, no matter how hard I try. I shake the unwanted images from my mind.

Absolutely not. I won't go there even in fantasy. These men are practically animals. They aren't exactly known for being gentle or considerate lovers. I'll die before I let that animal touch me. And honestly that's a possibility anyway. It's not as though no valkyrie ever died at the hands of her mate. There are stories. I'm determined not to be one of those cautionary tales.

I use the hotel's wireless internet to find a flight. Beauvais-Tillé Airport has a flight out in four hours. That's eighty-five kilometers from here. I'm used to America. We do miles. The metric system is practically a foreign language. I'm far better with French than with Kilometers. I think I can get there in time to go through airport security and have time left to unwind in the private lounge —a perk of my platinum card.

I'm not exactly poor, but at the same time literally staying in the air flying nonstop more or less for weeks would be a serious financial drain on most people—even if I fly coach. I have truly fallen into a hell dimension... fear of flying? Let's just fly over international waters for weeks on end. No problem!

But every petty fear I have pales in comparison to the berserker.

CHLOE

It's been a week of nonstop flying. Trying to sleep in coach was too much so I had to switch to first class three days into this insanity. I'm spending so much money that I'm at least able to use frequent flier miles to cover some of it, but it's still goodbye savings, hello new and exciting poverty. I've circled the globe a few times already. And all I can say is... my body feels weird. Humans, and apparently also valkyries, are not meant to be in the air for this long.

I'm about to get on a flight to Seoul flying out from Belgium when I'm stopped at the gate.

"Ms. Chloe Penn?"

"Y-yes?" I say hesitantly as he scrutinizes my boarding pass.

"I'm sorry but you're on our no-fly list."

"I... what? Why?" Does Belgium even *have* a no-fly list? I thought that was an American thing. I mean I guess reasonably every country could have such a thing or maybe it's an airport specific thing for this airline.

"I'm afraid I don't have the details but we'll have to ask you to leave."

"I... but what about... I bought a ticket. I was given a boarding pass!" I snatch the pass from his hand and wave it around as if he needs this demonstration with props.

"I understand. It was a mistake. There was a glitch and... you'll be refunded your ticket price but I'm going to have to ask you to leave the airport now."

He glances pointedly at security who seem prepared to forcibly have me removed from the premises if I don't comply with their request. I do because I can't afford to be detained or waste time. I need to get somewhere where I can use the wi-fi, find another airport, buy another ticket, and get back in the air as quickly as possible.

But what if I'm on other lists? Maybe I should have planned this more carefully. Maybe there should have been a pattern, like I was flying for business or something. But even those traveling for business don't stay in the air constantly. All my life I've been afraid of flying, but this past week I've been terrified of my feet touching solid ground.

And then sometimes I'm afraid of flying for different reasons. I've had nightmares the past several days of him finding me, him being on the same flight and cornering me in the air where there's no place to run. Only one of the dreams had a happy ending... I sprouted huge black wings and flew out the emergency exit. Then I woke on the floor of the plane... turbulence.

I still have just the one bag of luggage, which has proven pretty useful in the sense of it's easier to be on the run with one bag than with many. I've been buying clothes to change into in airport shops, and throwing the old ones away because there's no place for me to wash them. I can't be on the ground that long.

I'm not sure how the berserkers track. I don't know if it's by psychic link or by smell. I wonder if he's found all the places I've been simply by tracking the scent of the clothing I've had to leave behind.

The first clothes were the hardest to throw away. They were favorite outfits that I wanted to bring specifically with me to Paris, but I needed the room in my bag. The rest have been easy: stupid airport and city-specific tourist T-shirts, shorts, underwear—things I can easily part with. Luckily I've been able to shower in the nicer lounges.

It's extremely crowded outside the airport and there are no taxis available so I just start walking as quickly as possible across the open field. It feels far too exposed, but it's the fastest way to get to a row of shops I spot in the distance and a coffee shop with the possibility of wi-fi so I can create a new flight plan.

The sun has recently set, and I've only gone a few yards when the sky opens up and the rain starts. I take off in a run to get out of the downpour. It's coming down so hard I can barely see a foot in front of me. I duck my head to keep the water from getting into my eyes. It's a large spongey-soft field of grass. I've decided I can keep my head down and run until I reach pavement. But instead I run right into a solid wall of muscle.

"E-excuse me," I say with chattering teeth, my voice hidden behind a loud crack of thunder. I look up as lightning illuminates both the sky and the man's face.

The berserker.

"C-Cade?" I say, hopeful, even though I know it's not Cade. The human side would never be able to track me, and he wouldn't have a reason or desire to.

He speaks low to me in Old Norse. The old language—which I never bothered to learn—rolls over me in a menacing wave of dark promises I'm able to remain ignorant of a little while longer due to our language barrier.

Lucky me.

He wears a long-sleeved shirt, completely soaked through by the rain which doesn't seem to trouble him. I can't use my magic unless I have bare skin to touch. And it has to be his chest—over his heart.

I stumble back, turn, and run. But the ground is too wet, rivers of mud flowing out in all directions. My feet slip out from under me, and I go down hard. I'm lying on my back, my breath coming out in harsh gasps as the rain pelts down. I try to scan the field to find him, but it's so dark. Another flash of lightning allows me to see a dark looming shadow a moment before he's on me.

The berserker straddles my slight form. He's so big next to me, so overwhelming and oppressively large. And now I'm having a panic attack because who wouldn't have a panic attack in this situation? He could just as easily kill me if I can't calm him.

"Please," I beg. "Please let me go. You don't want to hurt me. Please."

There's this part of me that wants to insist I'm his mate as though this might buy me protection instead of a far darker fate. At best it might buy me temporary relief. But I know he sees the mark, smells it, feels it. As if to prove this, he leans down and sniffs at my throat. A low rumbling growl starts, and I shudder as his warm tongue runs over my skin.

I can't stop the tears. Even if I could somehow get away from him, what he's doing right now? It's only making the mark stronger. If I escaped him again how long would I have to elude him this time for it to fade? Maybe it's too late, and there's nothing I can do. Maybe his tongue on my throat just sealed my fate.

I've never heard of any valkyrie getting away from a berserker a second time after the mark has been reinforced. It may only be possible after that initial preliminary claim. I wish my mother had bothered to tell me more than *Run*.

Is he going to just rip my clothes off and take me right here in this field? I struggle against him and against my own increasingly vivid and inappropriate fantasies. He growls as if reprimanding me, like I'm the one being unreasonable here.

"Get OFF me!" I shriek.

And it truly is a valkyrie shriek. It's an ear-splitting sound that has never come out of my mouth before. It's something so much more than human.

More lightning. This time I have the strange feeling the streak that just lit up the sky was me.

The berserker finally gets up and pulls me to stand with him. He grips my wrists together in one hand and barks a sharp order in Old Norse.

I feel the anger radiating off him. He's not exactly in a full berserker rage but he *is* the berserker right now. As if there could be any doubt after he just growled and licked me. I feel the otherworldly energy crackling off him, the edges of his control fraying with each second of his escalating agitation.

"I'm not yours! You have to let me go." I scream at him, trying to replicate that shriek again, but it just comes out sounding like a human scream. And there's nobody crazy enough to be out in this storm but us, so the scream isn't even useful on that level.

I don't know if he understands me since he continues to speak in the old language. Then he's dragging me across the field back toward the airport.

"Where are you taking me? I'm on the no-fly list... they won't let me fly! You can't take me on a plane. Please... Cade... Cade you don't want to do this."

I don't even really know what he's planning. Actually yes I do. From the moment he started speaking to me, I've felt the mark burning to life against my throat. I can feel it's energetic glow as it seems to leap in excitement at the return of the one who created it. I may not be eager to become his eternally bound mate, but the mark is.

The mud cakes on my shoes so thick I can barely move to keep up with him. We don't stop until we reach a jet at a private hangar, partly fenced off from the rest of the airport. I have no idea how we're not going through airport security right now or how he has a jet. Does Cade have a jet or does the berserker have a jet?

The pilots speak to Cade in Old Norse. Are they berserkers, too? I'm so confused about what's happening right now.

Cade barks an order at me that I'm sure is the equivalent of

"Go, Now!" I guess some things sound sort of the same in any language. Suddenly I'm stumbling up the stairs to get into the aircraft. Once inside he points at a chair, and I sit in it. I can't make myself stop shaking. If the others are berserkers, too... What if they have a freak out? Could they be something else besides berserkers? They're obviously *other* and from our dimension, or it's doubtful they'd be fluently speaking the old language.

Why didn't I listen to my mother and learn Old Norse? *It's a dead language*, I said. And learning it might have given me a better chance of not ending up dead, too.

How does he have all this? The jet? The... staff? I don't understand. I was sure he was newly changed. He felt young... fresh... newly born. Unless all of this belongs to Cade, but why would the pilots be speaking the old language? And how would the berserker know Cade had all this? I admit I'm not entirely clear on how much the human side and the berserker side know and intermix. Are there two separate souls inhabiting the same body? Is it like a split personality? Like a Jeckyll and Hyde sort of deal?

"Cade, please, please calm down."

He looms over me, breathing hard, his eyes flashing quickly back and forth from gold to blue as though he can't control the change, which doesn't inspire a lot of confidence for my future with this guy. His hair drips water down the harsh planes of his face. The edges of fangs peek out from between his lips. His hands clench and unclench at his sides making his muscles seem even more dramatic pushing against his soaked-through shirt.

Oh my god, Chloe! Stop thinking about him that way.

Of all the moments to feel attraction to someone, my libido has the worst timing, and the worst taste in the world. I may as well start dating serial killers.

He growls as he stares into my eyes. It takes everything in me not to look away, but I'm afraid if I do I'll only register as easier prey in his mind. Maybe I shouldn't have run. Maybe I should have let him catch me when he was more human and I could have reasoned with him. Berserkers don't inherently want to kill their mates, but if he's too far gone…

A rope seems to appear from nowhere, and then he's tying one of my wrists to the arm rest. The plane begins to taxi down the runway, and my panic climbs the more we pick up speed.

"Please, please don't tie me up. Please. I'm scared of flying, I can't…"

He laughs at this. Wait… does he understand me? If he understands me why won't he speak English? I don't completely blame him for the laughter. I mean… I *have* spent literally a week in the air almost nonstop. To say I'm scared of flying after all that seems frankly insane. But nobody tied me up for those other flights, and this somehow makes everything more scary because if we do start to crash… there's nothing I can do. Not that anyone has a great deal of control in a plane crash. But still.

He pulls his shirt over his head, and my breath stops for a moment as I'm confronted once again with that beautiful muscled, tattooed chest. He takes my free hand and presses it over the viking tattoo, taking a long, deep breath.

Before he can switch fully back to Cade—if Cade is even still in there—he pulls my hand away and ties it to the other arm rest and goes to buckle himself into his own seat across from mine.

The flight is long and tense, at least from my perspective. But he doesn't do anything violent or unpredictable, and aside from when he pressed my hand to his chest to calm down, he hasn't touched me again. He growls softly. Or maybe that's a purr. I can't be sure. His eyes remain gold now, his fangs a prominent and ever-present threat. But he just watches me.

THE BERSERKER

(A ROUGH TRANSLATION FROM OLD NORSE)

She's lucky I took her when I did. For her sake. A week was too long to go without her touch. I was on the brink of losing control. Tracking her wasn't the problem. She was easy enough to track with the link we share. I always knew where she was. She's clever though—staying in the air.

If berserkers tracked by scent, she would have had a chance. On a certain level it doesn't really matter if the creature who can calm our rage is especially intelligent, but given our link to Odin... when we aren't in a rage, we appreciate a woman with brains—not just a pretty face. During our time apart I discovered her name: Chloe. It's as lovely and delicate as she is, like a flower blooming after a spring rain.

She's been crying for the past two hours almost non-stop, as if she thinks she can appeal to my mercy. She must really not know what a berserker is, which is odd for a valkyrie. I could understand if a human didn't know. Did they keep this girl locked away in a convent? Oh... we've got some memories in the collective about convents... back when every human knew who we were and cowered in terror, praying for their god to save them from the wrath of the North Men.

"Cade, you have to turn the plane around and let me go. Please. You can't take me anywhere anyway. Think about it. How will you get me through customs? Maybe I didn't have to go through airport security for the jet, but... we'll have to go through customs in any country we enter. You know that, right?"

Cade. It's as I thought. She's trying to appeal to the human. I've maintained control so the human can't come out until I'm ready for him to come out. And what she doesn't realize yet is that eventually Cade will become a bit more animal and will see things my way. She doesn't have the ally in the human she thinks she has. At least she won't have him for long.

I just growl at her because it's pointless speaking to her in the old language. How does she *not* know our language? I want to tie her up and punish her for that.

"You *can* understand me!" There's accusation and hurt in her tone like I'm just doing this to be a bastard.

I'm starting to get bits of Cade's language memory, but we're only at the listening comprehension phase of things in this soul and memory merging process. I'm not yet at a point where I can actually speak it. And my native language feels more natural. I should make her learn Old Norse if she wants to communicate with me so badly.

My gaze rakes slowly over her. I'm sure we'll communicate just fine... horizontally. She flushes under my gaze and looks away.

In truth, I actually don't have to take her through customs. I have an arrangement. One of our guys. Berserkers have disappeared off the radar for a reason. Most in this dimension have a valkyrie mate who keeps them sane, and the collective soul we share makes it possible for us to communicate telepathically across great distances.

Even though she's easy enough to track, I wasn't yet at liberty to go run her down. I had to arrange a place to take her first. Another of my kind was decent enough to loan me his chateau in the French countryside, his jet, and a few members of his staff for as long as I need all of them.

I could make this quick and easy. I could have taken her and completed the claim out in the rain, but she's my mate. When I'm thinking clearly, I am disinclined to harm her or take her in a field somewhere like some rutting animal.

For her sake, I hope she gives in to me before my control slips. It was too easy to hold her down, too easy to prevent her from taking the necessary action to calm me. Her influence has too many limitations for her own safety.

4

CHLOE

I know he understands me. His face showed too much recognition when I spoke, but he still refuses to speak to me in English. When we land—I have no idea where—Cade gets off the plane, leaving me behind. One of the pilots comes back to where I'm seated, still tied to the chair.

"It will be best for you if you don't struggle or fight him."

I flinch at these words even as I'm surprised and grateful to hear my own language.

"Why won't he speak to me?" I sound like a petulant child, even to my own ears. But I mean if this cretin is going to kidnap me and I don't know, force me to be his mate, he at least owes me the courtesy of more than grunts and growls and barking at me in a language I don't understand.

"I'm not at liberty to talk about that," he says.

"What about customs? How does he think he's getting me through customs?"

"It's been handled." I have no idea what that's supposed to mean, but it's the only answer I'm getting. He unties my hands and guides me out of the plane to the waiting black car. I think it's a Bentley but I don't know enough about cars to be sure. Either way, it's nice—far too nice for a guy who just got to this dimension a week ago.

I'm surprised the berserker isn't in the back of the car waiting for me. He's not in the front of the car, either.

"Where's Cade?" I ask, not knowing what else to call him.

The driver meets my eyes through the rearview mirror. "He took a separate car." The engine starts and the locks go down as the car pulls forward.

The driver doesn't elaborate any further on this situation, but the look in his eyes when they meet mine in the mirror are heavy with meaning, like a clearly printed out message I can easily read. The message is... *He doesn't trust himself in a space this small with you.*

I can't express how warm and fuzzy and protected that *doesn't* make me feel. Does the berserker not trust himself not to fuck me or not to kill me? The jet was an enclosed space, but it's true this is much tighter. And there were other people on the jet—or other berserkers. I'm still not clear on that part.

I let out a long slow breath. "You have to let me go. He'll kill me."

"He doesn't wish to kill you."

His reply sounds as though he's not sure it's entirely in the berserker's control whether he kills me or just keeps me forever like a possessive dog with a favorite bone.

"Let me go!" I say more forcefully. I'm not sure if I can open the car door from the inside, but we're moving too fast down the road for it to be safe for me to escape this way anyway. We're also out in the middle of nowhere, driving through the sprawling French countryside. So where in the hell would I go? He'd find me. My chances of escape are even smaller now than they were the first time.

"I'm afraid that won't be possible. I was given very explicit instructions."

There's no emotional tone change. Everything the driver says sounds professional as if he's transported berserker hostages hundreds of times. And maybe he has.

A part of me wants to scream, kick the seats, do *something*, but I can't see how these actions could possibly improve my situation. I could cry and panic, but I can't work it up. I know I'm in so much trouble, and the window for my escape shrinks with every moment that passes, but the deepest problem of this situation is my physical attraction to the monster who marked me.

I feel the burn under my skin, as though the mark knows when I'm thinking about it. The mark is on the berserker's side in this disagreement, not mine. My body is quickly moving to the berserker's side as well.

I don't bother asking where I'm being taken. I'm sure the driver would give me another robotic professional non-answer. I spot a bottle of champagne chilling in a bucket of ice on the floor next to the seat beside me. I'm not sure what the purpose of the champagne is or if it's meant for me or someone else, and honestly I don't fucking care. It's alcohol, and that suddenly sounds like a super good idea to me.

Since I've decided I'm not going to have some meltdown in the back seat, begging is pointless, and flinging myself out of a vehicle flying down a long abandoned road at a brisk clip isn't an option... getting drunk seems like the most reasonable thing to do.

I pull off the shiny light blue foil from the top and pop the cork. I try to aim it in such a way so as not to have it bounce back and hit me, but it's a small space and I have to duck as it flies back at me, narrowly missing my face.

The driver arches a brow at me through the mirror but otherwise makes no comment about my life choices. I'm only able to drink enough to give me a bit of a buzz before we reach a stately chateau. Castle might actually be a better word for it.

I pull the bottle away from my lips just long enough to gape out the window like the tourist I am as we drive up. It's huge, weathered brown stone, and very very old. And there are towers. An entire retinue of guards lines the front of this possibly-castle.

The driver parks the car, comes around, and opens the door, offering a hand to help me. I stumble out... maybe just slightly more drunk than I thought. But it's probably for the best. Where the hell could I ever run from this man? My fate feels sealed. And once the mating is complete won't I be safe then?

I shake my head, trying to clear these insane thoughts. No, no mating! There can be no mating with a berserker. It's the alcohol talking. But it isn't just my head feeling buzzy. Images of Cade without a shirt from the first time I saw him flash into my mind, and now other parts of me feel buzzy. More exciting, intimate parts. And it's at this point I realize I haven't had an orgasm since before the first time I saw him—all the fleeing and the endless international flights can really kill a girl's mojo after all.

A couple of the guards step out from the line and approach me. One takes the bottle of champagne gently from my hand and places it on the ground.

The berserker's men lead me inside, down several long hallways, and down a flight of steps into what can only be described as a dungeon—so... castle, then? They don't say a word as they toss me into a surprisingly posh cell—as cells go. There's a glassed-in shower, sink, and a toilet, that while simple, don't look gross. The cell also contains a very large actually comfortable looking bed. There's a sizable slot in the door where food can be passed through. This makes me hopeful that he's not planning to starve me at least.

I could do the cliché thing and bang on the door and demand they let me out, but I know that's pointless. This is pretty well orchestrated. No one is letting me out. All I can do is pace and wait for the berserker, trying to pretend that idea doesn't excite me even as it upsets me.

I don't have to wait long. A few minutes later the door opens and the devil steps inside. He speaks in the old language to one of the men who brought me down here. The other man nods, then shuts the door and locks it, trapping me inside the cell with the berserker.

He says: "Cade" loudly, followed by a string of Old Norse. He doesn't seem to be speaking to me, but to the room in general. He speaks for a while as if he's giving out some kind of orders, but again, he's not looking at or speaking to me.

Finally he stops talking and his golden gaze lands on me. He growls. The growl seems sexual somehow, or maybe it's because of the way he's looking at me. I back away even though I know there's no place to go.

I hold my hands up in front of me and manage to stumble into the sink, banging my elbow against the stainless steel. That's probably going to bruise. "C-Cade. I-I don't know why you marked me but..."

He laughs.

Okay. I do know why he marked me. But I mean why me?

The berserker continues to advance. He pulls his T-shirt over his head. I've already admitted I'm attracted to him. Very shamefully attracted. But I can't be a berserker's mate. I can't be tied forever to a crazy guy who feels remorse for nothing. I'm sure he's killed in the week since we met. Probably a lot. I'm about to start crying. I feel the tears welling up. I'm not sure if it's some weird side effect from the alcohol or the fact that I can't be tied forever to a murderer, and this is suddenly getting very real. And why didn't I just fling myself out of the moving car while I had the chance?

"Cade, don't do this... I don't want... I can't... I can't be your mate... just let the mark fade and let me go... please..."

He ignores me and grabs my wrist, pressing my palm hard against his chest. He holds it there much longer this time. His intense erratic heartbeat pounds wildly against my hand, giving away just how unhinged he is, how little control he truly has. But finally, after several minutes it slows to a cadence I recognize as normal.

Every time he does this, it gets easier for me to dissipate his fury. It doesn't stick to me or affect my own mood like it did the first time. It's like my powers activated and my body figured out what to do with it. Maybe I've turned into some sort of berserker fury garbage disposal.

His eyes shift to blue and he stumbles back away from me.

"Cade?"

The man who looks up at me doesn't have the wildness nor that sense of possession in his eyes. Instead he looks guilty and like he might be sick.

"I understand now why you ran from me when we got off the plane. You knew more about what I am than I did."

This isn't the berserker talking. This is the guy I met that first night on the plane after I calmed him down. He begins to pace, running a hand through his long dark blonde hair.

"I have to get you out of here, you have no idea the things he wants to do to you."

"Y-you know what he has planned?"

Cade looks up at me, pain radiating from his face and nods. "I've mostly just been able to watch from inside him, but I can sometimes hear his thoughts."

"They're in English?" Because if this asshole is thinking in English and speaking in Old Norse I might transform into a proper valkyrie and go on my own rampage.

Cade shakes his head. "No. Old Norse. But I understand him. I can't speak it but I can understand it. I'm not sure if that makes sense or not. I'm also getting some of his memories."

Could that be what's happening to the berserker as well? He understands English but can't speak it?

"What did he say before he left and let you come out?"

"He said to tell you that you will stay in this cell until the mating bond is complete and that when he comes back he'll be able to speak English."

"He said more than that," I counter.

Cade looks away from me, a mix of shame and disgust on his face.

"What else did he say?"

There's a long silence. Finally Cade sighs. "He said he'd be willing to share you with me and that I should soften you up for him, seduce you so you're more... receptive."

I have a feeling Cade is giving me a gentleman's version of the berserker's words. Even so, my body responds as though this were the most stimulating idea in the world.

"Are you supposed to stay in here until the mating is complete, too?" I mean obviously his physical body must be here for us to mate, but I'm wondering if he has to stay the entire time. It's only me who truly has to be contained until it's complete, after all.

Cade shrugs. "I don't know. I don't think he plans to come back until we've bonded somehow. Anyway, I don't have a key."

"Can't you control it? Keep him away? I mean, there's nothing to make you angry here. The berserker is fueled on rage."

Cade begins to pace. "It's not like that. I've been out a few times in the past week and I'm starting to remember more. On the airplane—the first time it happened—I wasn't angry about anything. The berserker rose up and then decided *he* was angry. I don't know if there's a trigger. He just seems to come out whenever he feels like it."

"Has he killed?" I don't know why I ask this. I don't want to know, and anyway I already know. It's what they do.

Cade looks away. "It was bad. You can't be tied to this demon, Chloe."

Technically berserkers aren't demons, but I'm pretty sure Cade is just being metaphorical. And now I'm tripping over the fact that he just said my name, and it sounds warm and rich and nice on his tongue. I wish he was a regular guy because aside from the crazy passenger he's got riding attached to his soul, he is completely my type.

"Do you know how you became a berserker?"

Part of me thinks it somehow magically happened just from the way he looks. He looks like he belongs to another time... a viking time. The ice blue eyes. That body. The long dark blond hair. The tattoos. Any woman with a pulse would want to hop on that and take a ride. I might too, if I wasn't afraid the berserker would choose that moment to rise up and finish marking me and tying me to him forever. The stakes are a little high to give in to my hormones right now.

He sighs and runs a hand through his hair. "It's the new tattoo. The one with the..."

"I know which one," I say, interrupting him. I'd wondered if it was the tattoo.

"I'm not a berserker," he says. "The berserker is inside me, but it's not me. I'm a separate person. He's hitchhiking in my body."

"I'm sorry." It's all I know to say. Cade seems too broken from what he's witnessed his body do the past week to say anything more.

5

THE BERSERKER

(A ROUGH TRANSLATION FROM OLD NORSE)

I wait until they fall asleep to emerge. It's easiest when Cade sleeps. He's lately taken to trying to fight me when he feels me rise up, and though I'm strong enough to best him, I've resisted the urge. If I fight him I could lose control before I'm ready. I could hurt her. But after the most recent exposure to Chloe's touch, I'm still calm enough to think and strategize.

I wake on the floor of the cell. Cade decided to be a gentleman and let Chloe have the bed. Hmmm. They didn't even look under the bed. I'm so disappointed by this. Don't captives normally explore their cage better? It looks like I'll have to raise the stakes myself. I'm careful and quiet so I don't wake the girl as I pull out all the things I've stored under the bed. There are towels for the shower as well as a large black satin-covered box.

The box is six feet by four feet with plenty of room for all my toys. I stack the towels next to the shower and lay all the toys out in easy view. Then I strip my clothes off and shove them through the food slot in the door for a guard to pick up.

Chloe sleeps deeply, far more deeply than she has the right to with the threat I present. Her chest rises and falls gently. I slowly pull back the blanket. She sleeps in only a London Bridge T-shirt and a pair of innocent white panties.

It takes all my self control not to bury my head between her legs and let her wake to learn why she doesn't want to fight me. I know she's attracted even though she doesn't want to be. I smell it on her. I smell the perfume of her desire even now, and I wonder if she's dreaming of me or of Cade.

CHLOE

I shiver as cool air hits my skin. I'm about to reach to pull the covers up when I realize I'm bound. My eyes shoot open, and I look wildly around the room. Cade still sleeps on the floor, but he's naked with his clothes nowhere to be found. I'm naked, too, my arms and legs spread wide and tied to the bed.

I want to call for help, but I'm not sure which one of them will wake up. And even if it's Cade, I don't want him to see me this way. Then I realize... the berserker saw me this way. How could I have slept through him undressing me? Did he... touch me in my sleep?

I'm sure if he'd done more, he wouldn't have been able to stop himself from completing the mating bond. And I'm sure I'd know if he'd done that.

Oh crap, I need to pee. I really really hope it's Cade that wakes up.

"Cade!" My entire body blushes as I realize not only is Cade going to see this, but the berserker will get to see it again from inside Cade. After yesterday I now understand they're both always there, it's just that one of them is in the driver's seat and the other has to watch. Or maybe *gets to watch* in the case of the berserker.

"Cade!" I say louder.

He jumps up, his head whipping around as though he's expecting to be attacked. It takes him a moment to realize his clothes are gone. He sees me chained to the bed, and immediately his dick goes hard at the sight, his blue eyes darkening with lust. My body responds to his response, and I know that if he decided to ignore the better angels of his nature, there would be no resistance as my body opened to allow him to slide easily inside.

"C-Cade?" The look he's giving me makes me not entirely sure it's him.

He shakes himself out of his immediate carnal reaction and looks away. "I-I'm sorry."

"Could you untie me, please?"

"Yes... I ... yes of course." He walks to me awkwardly trying to avoid looking at me even as his body displays his arousal.

He pulls the sheet up to cover me before going to work freeing my ankles and wrists.

"I'm going to take a shower," he says when he's finished untying me.

"I'll look the other direction," I say.

"Thanks."

But he isn't as shy as I am, so I think he said it out of awkwardness and just not knowing what else to say.

I don't see my clothes anywhere, because of course the berserker took them away. All I have is the sheet to cover myself with. I would feel completely exposed and unsafe except that I don't feel unsafe with Cade. It's only what's living inside him that concerns me.

I face away from the shower and listen as the water runs. I do so well for about five minutes, and then I can't help it, I look. Cade faces the wall, the hot water sliding down his perfect body. There isn't enough steam to hide the view from me, and then I realize he's not showering.

One hand is braced against the wall, and although I can't see it, I can tell from the movement in his other arm that he's jerking off. I know when he's finished, not because he stops moving, but because of the soft shuddering sigh that leaves his mouth, barely louder than the spray of the water. Then he does grab the soap and showers. I could turn away now, but I find myself mesmerized by the soap suds sliding down his golden back. I unconsciously bite my lip. It's embarrassing how much I want to join him in the shower and beg him to take me.

I know he wants to. I just witnessed the evidence of it. And maybe he's not ready to go again, but he could take care of *me*. I'm sure he wouldn't mind. I'm sure he'd enjoy it. And maybe by the time he'd satisfied me, he'd be ready to... I shake the thoughts from my head.

What the hell? That's not me. I feel the burn underneath the skin of my neck and I reach up to touch it. I expect it to burn my fingertips but the feeling is all on the inside. Is it the mark making me feel this way? Making me think this way? It has to be.

Cade shuts off the water, and I turn away quickly so he doesn't catch me. But I know he'll catch me the second he sees my face again. I'm a terrible liar—even when the lies are silent. Maybe especially when they're silent.

"What the fuck?" he says when he gets out of the shower. But he says it in a casual tone, not exactly like an accusation. Still, I feel accused.

"What?" I say, still looking away.

"I'm in a towel, you can look," Cade says.

"I don't think I can." Because Cade wrapped in a towel feels somehow even more dangerous to my quickly fraying sanity than him standing there totally naked. Wrapped in a towel, there's mystery and temptation, and I can't pretend I somehow find his erection threatening instead of exciting if he's safely tucked away behind cotton.

"This," he says. And I swear I can *feel* him pointing. "Did you see this shit?"

I finally turn to find out what he's talking about, and that's when I notice the box for the first time. It's giant and black and looks like it must have been under the bed. It's short enough to slide under, and where else would it have been? I know it wasn't out here last night. Seriously, they should put me in a detective show. Marvel at my amazing deductive reasoning.

I feel my face go red at the contents of the box, and at least now Cade won't know I watched him in the shower because there are plenty of new reasons for my awkwardness and blushing.

"This is for you." Cade says, disgust dripping from his voice as he hands me a cream-colored envelope with my name neatly printed on the back.

I know the disgust is aimed at our captor, not at me. Even so, I feel guilty of something.

I take the envelope from him and gingerly slide my finger underneath the flap, freeing a red wax seal. The paper is thick and expensive with a watermark from a high-end stationery brand. It seems far too refined and civilized for the monster it comes from. But then again so was the jet, the car, his home.

My dearest Chloe,

Please accept these gifts for your pleasure. I know you feel my mark calling to you to accept me. I'll let you practice with the human for the short time he remains so. One of my associates translated this for me, but soon I'll be able to communicate freely with you. Give me a good show. I'll be watching with rapt attention.

Cade

I read the letter five times because I can't bring myself to look up at Cade. The berserker signed Cade's name. Maybe he has no name of his own. Maybe Cade *is* his name now. I feel his eyes on me—not Cade—the berserker. I'd forgotten he was here with us.

If he thinks I'm going to use anything in that box, he's out of his mind. The box is filled to the brim with sex toys. Penetrating things. Vibrating things. Silk scarves, cuffs, whips, floggers, lingerie, *edible* things. It's like a kinky honeymoon kit, and I shudder as I realize that's exactly how the berserker sees this.

To him this is our *honeymoon*.

Before I can get too freaked out about this, there's a knock on the door. Um? It's not like we can just open it and let somebody in, but the person on the other side is only announcing breakfast I guess because two trays are slid through the slot. Cade grabs them and places them on the floor between us. We sit down with our legs crossed, both of us studiously ignoring the black box of carnality.

The trays are the same as middle school plastic lunch trays with the different sized rectangles and squares for different foods. On each tray is scrambled eggs, fried ham, buttered toast, and half an orange. Though Cade's portions of both eggs and ham are much bigger than mine. To drink, we each have both a carton of whole milk and a carton of orange juice.

At least I don't have to worry about poisoning. The berserker wouldn't poison himself, and he thinks I'm his mate.

"So," Cade says... "you're a valkyrie?"

I want to ask how he knows this but of course he knows because he's been connected up to the berserker's mind somehow.

"Yeah," I say, not sure what else to say.

"And he thinks you're his mate?"

I shrug. "I guess so. He marked me."

An angry expression crosses Cade's face, and for a moment I think he's turning back into the berserker, but he's just reacting to what I said. "Where?"

"It's not visible. It's an... energetic... a magic thing. It's hard to explain."

"Oh." He takes a few bites of ham. "Hey can you open this carton for me, I always mess them up."

"Sure." I take both of his cartons and open them. It almost makes me laugh because girls are always asking guys to open jars and stuff. But it's true, these milk cartons take finesse and smaller hands. I pass the perfectly opened cartons back to him.

"Thanks." He closes his juice back up and shakes it. I'm not sure if this is entirely necessary. But you never know with orange juice. Sometimes if you don't shake it up you end up getting what tastes like barely orange flavored water at the start and then at the end it's like a Sweet Tart. So better safe than sorry.

We eat in silence for several minutes, both of us no doubt trying not to think about all the disturbing aspects of our captivity together. Finally he says, "So, can you explain what's happening to me?"

"I... what do you mean?" How does he not get it yet? He's been in some kind of mind link with the berserker for over a week now.

As if reading *my* mind, Cade says, "It's not as though he sits around thinking about his own origin story or talks to his friends about it. It's information they already know."

Fair enough. I hadn't thought of it that way. "To be honest with you, I'm not the best person to ask. My mother didn't really tell me much about berserkers. I just know about the rages and that you guys are dangerous and to run if I see one, though that's useless information now," I say, gesturing at the four walls of our cell.

Cade looks hurt by this. "I would never harm you."

"You know it's not you I'm worried about." There's a chance the actual berserker wouldn't harm me, either, but that doesn't mean I want to be eternally tied to him.

"So you don't know anything?" he presses.

"Well I mean, I could tell you about our world, where we come from."

"Okay." He's somehow gotten through his entire breakfast and orange juice and is probably one big gulp away from finishing the milk which looks comically tiny in his big hand.

"So I guess with your tattoo you're at least familiar with Norse mythology, right?"

"Right. I'm not an expert, but I know all the basic stories."

"Okay, so, spoiler alert, they aren't myths. Actually some of them are. It's complicated. The point is, these stories are at least partly inspired by real things. But time runs really differently here than it does there. Do you know the story where Odin goes to the seer and learns the prophecy of Ragnarok?"

"Yeah, in the Voluspa," he says, and I'm sure he's trying to impress me right now by knowing the name of the first and most famous poem in this dimension's written down lore. And to be honest, I *am* a little impressed.

"Part of that happened about a year ago. Time moves *really* differently. So some of the stories are true but happened very recently at least in that dimension. Some of the stories are totally made up. Humans take the inspiration and make it their own. And some of them are sort of channeled prophecies. There are seers on this plane who don't know they're seers and don't realize there are prophetic truths in their art. So any one of the stories here that hasn't actually happened in my world, *could* still happen. Or some version of it could happen. And I'm sure Odin has been trying to figure out which of the many stories could be prophecies for his dimension. The possibility of Ragnorak being the highest concern because... spoiler alert, Odin doesn't survive that battle. So he's pretty motivated to get his army together."

"Wow. If you'd told me that on the plane when we met I would have thought you were crazy."

I'm staring at the tattoo that somehow made him a berserker. "I wish I could read runes, I would love to know what your tattoo says."

"It says *Forever pledged to Odin.*"

Great. Of course it does. But I don't comment because he's already a berserker, and it's not as though anything can be done about it now.

"Not that long ago, in my dimension's time, people here believed in and prayed to what are now thought of as *the old gods*. Odin is still collecting warriors, but most of the men in this world have become pretty uninspiring over the past thousand years."

"Are all of Odin's warriors berserkers?" Cade asks.

I shake my head, still eating my breakfast. "No. Most of the warriors in Valhalla are regular men. Though a lot of the vikings were berserkers. Think of berserkers as the equivalent of Seal Team Six, compared to the regular recruits."

"So how does being pledged to Odin turn one into a berserker?"

I shrug because really his guess is as good as mine. There were plenty of men pledged to Odin who didn't become berserkers. And I've never been fully clear on how Odin specifically fits in. Is he part of the same larger berserker hive mind? Is he the origin of it, creating little pieces of himself to amass an elite fighting unit? I truly have no idea.

It's as shrouded in mystery to me as where valkyries come from. But I feel a bit better about it since humans don't fully understand their own origins either. They have different stories about it like this god or that god made them, or evolution, or... but who really knows anything at the end of the day? A lot about life is a mystery no matter where you come from or what you are. A lot of this stuff is just comforting bedtime stories we tell ourselves.

He takes a deep breath and finally asks the question I know he's been wanting to ask. "How do I undo it? It's like a curse right? So we just break the curse and..."

I shake my head. "It's not like that. It's... The only way to get rid of him is to die, but then you're dead. So... maybe not the kind of freedom you're looking for."

CADE

There's a long uncomfortable silence as she seems to have run out of things to say. "So, how long have you been in this dimension?" I ask. I still feel crazy talking about this magic stuff, but I've seen too much by now to deny it.

"Oh, I was born here, a long time ago. I visited the other world once and stayed long enough that when I got back here we'd somehow gone from tribal cultures living in the frozen forest to... the internet. It took a while to adjust and so I haven't been back."

Her gaze keeps shifting uncomfortably to the black box and then sliding back to me.

"Stop looking at the box, Chloe. I'm not him, and I'm not going to do those things to you."

"Y-you're not?"

I'm not going to force myself on her to *soften her up* for the monster lurking inside me, no. But I don't use those words. I just shake my head.

"Do you not want to?"

I hear the insecurity in her voice, as if she isn't the most perfect fucking creature I could ever be blessed to be trapped with. If I were just a little less noble, there would be no hesitation.

"Oh honey, if these were different circumstances I'd have you bent over a counter or desk or random table by now. But you can't really say you want to be here with me. We're not exactly on a date."

She bites her lip and looks away. But I caught her. I saw the way she was looking at me. I probably *could* have her right now, and she'd willingly come to me. But the problem is... that plays right into the berserker's hands, and when he comes out, he won't be so gentle with her.

I don't know how long I can hold him back. It destroys me thinking of what my body may do to her when the berserker gets free, of what I'll have to watch my body doing to her with no way to save her, no way to stop him.

Maybe we should... maybe I *should* soften her up. Maybe it would be easier for her then. I've already examined every square inch of this cell and we aren't getting out until the berserker is ready for us to get out, until this girl is tied to him forever.

Well, it looks like neither one of us is going to escape. If that's the case, won't she and I eventually...? How many years will I be able to watch him take her without wanting to hold her and comfort her, without wanting to try to give her something soft and loving to make up for whatever brutality may come from him?

But won't she just look into my eyes and see the monster instead of the man? Once that bridge has been crossed? Maybe her first memory with this body should be sweet, soft, romantic. But no matter how I rationalize it in my mind, I can't do it. I can't go there.

The energy between us feels heavy with tension and awkwardness. I haven't felt this uncomfortable in the presence of a beautiful woman since I was a teenager. I just don't know how to make this better, and I'm afraid anything I do or say can only make it worse. So I try to distract her with funny stories about my childhood, hoping against hope that one or both of us will find the will to take comfort from each other so at least we have that, and not just the monster between us.

But I'm sure if we consummate this twisted joining, the berserker will use that moment of unguarded pleasure to come out and claim her. And then it's somehow my fault. If I let myself go inside of her, he'll use that moment of weakness to break free.

He comes out often when I sleep. Maybe I should try to stay awake as long as possible. But I'm only delaying the inevitable. I'm convinced he'll either come out when I hit total exhaustion or when I'm unconscious. It doesn't buy her that much time.

The day drags forever. We have lunch in awkward silence. Finally I say... "You could chain me to the bed."

She blushes furiously, and her eyebrows raise. "W-what?"

And now I think I might be blushing because that wasn't how I meant to say that. "I meant, you could chain me up at night while I sleep, so if he comes back you'll be safe. I can probably keep him at bay during the day."

She breaks down then, the tears flowing out of her so hard I wish I hadn't said anything at all. I want to go to her, hold her, comfort her. But I keep my distance.

She works to collect herself and looks up at me. "No. That won't work. You've been inside his head all this time, and you still don't understand how strong berserkers are. Those chains can't hold him. Nothing can hold him. They're too inhumanly strong. Even if it would work... even if you could keep him at bay... am I supposed to be locked in this cell for the rest of my life?"

She's right. The monster has already won. The only choice we get to make now is how we want to lose.

6

THE BERSERKER

(A ROUGH TRANSLATION FROM OLD NORSE)

This fucking human. I could strangle the shit out of him, except it would do me no good. Then I'd have lost a body and have to start over and I'm beginning to really enjoy inhabiting this body.

It's been four days. How can this guy be this goddamned noble? If I could punch him in the throat without feeling it myself, you can bet I'd do it. But the problem is, when I have control of the body, I feel it, not him.

I've stayed away because the entire point was that he'd get my mate comfortable. He'd play the good cop so that when I came out she'd be ready for me. I don't want to hurt her, but berserkers aren't exactly known for our self control.

She is naked. And he is naked. And they're locked in a cell! For fuck's sake, how does Cade make this situation complicated? He should have taken her already. Too late now. He's missed his window. It's my turn. Sorry, Chloe, but your first time will be with me, not the hero. I gave him a choice, and he chose wrong.

When Cade finally falls asleep, I take the opportunity to reclaim control. The red haze clouds my vision, and my gaze locks on her like a heat-seeking missile. Chloe tosses and turns in her sleep. I'm surprised she sleeps at all. I rip the blankets off, displaying that luscious perfect form. My mouth waters. I can't decide if I want to fucking eat her or claim her.

Sorry, kind of a bit of a wild animal here.

The lamp beside the bed is on. She can't sleep in the dark in this cell. Her eyes shoot open just as I realize I'm growling at her. She scrambles to sit up and looks for something to cover herself. When she spots the blankets at the other end of the room, she does the best she can to shield herself from me with her arms while twisting her body away.

She's still looking frantically around, and it occurs to me that she's expecting Cade to somehow pop out and rescue her. Oh my sweet girl, no, it's far too late for that romance hero nonsense.

"C-Cade?" she asks, her final attempt to deny the situation she finds herself in.

I shake my head slowly. "Guess again." She doesn't understand me. I'm still speaking in the old language. I need this part of the merge to complete so I can speak to her in a language she understands, but the magic decides how long the process takes, not me.

"Please... Cade... you can't... h-he hasn't softened me up yet. Y-you said..."

I just chuckle at this.

"I can't be your mate!" she shouts.

I want to tell her she already is. I can't let her go. The claim may not be fully forged, but we're already past the point of no return. I want to reassure her. I want to tell her she'll be safe with me, that eventually she'll be happy with me. But I don't have the words in English.

I'm barely holding onto control. Cade may not know it yet... but a bit at a time... parts of my essence are leaking into his. Parts of his essence are leaking into mine. I want to protect her. I want to love her. But the wildness that is the fundamental part of me wants to take her and mark her so savagely she never forgets who she belongs to.

I crook a finger at her and motion her to come to me. I can't use words to demand. I can't negotiate or argue with her. I cannot woo her. I need her to understand. I need her to come to me, to see the futility of trying to escape her destined mate. We are a story that was written before any human language, before time began.

We need to be joined. She needs to let go of the human she's been pretending to be and claim and awaken to the valkyrie she is. Valkyries and berserkers belong together. She could never be content with a weak human male. But someone didn't teach her right. Nature says she should respond to me, but her only response is fear.

If she'd learned the old language I could speak to her. It's only this long time with Cade that allows me to hold onto the thinnest thread of sanity. If I'd taken her from the start there would have been no words between us, not because of a language barrier, but because it would have been too primal. I wouldn't have been able to think in complete sentences, let alone speak.

I motion for her again.

She shakes her head.

"Chloe," I say. "Come." She only understands her name, of course. But my meaning is clear. She knows what I want.

Her gaze drifts down the length of my body to my erection. Yes, she knows what I want.

"I can't be your mate. I have a life. I have other things I want to do!"

Does she think I'm going to keep her locked up forever? That I would deny her whatever it is she wants to do? Unless what she wants to do is fuck someone else... Is that her only resistance?

"I can't be attached to a killer."

There it is.

I growl at her. She wasn't raised in our world. Her little visit notwithstanding. She was raised like a human. To think like a human. With the values and constricting morality of a human.

And until she releases that human lie, she will never fly free. I want to tell her these things, but I can't. I'm fucking trapped behind this language barrier. And the haze is getting stronger, the rage beginning to rise up, and if I don't take her soon, I might kill her.

And then I would never recover. I try to hold onto this reason to keep me from losing it and reigning down destruction. She is not something to kill. She is mine. A normal valkyrie wouldn't run from me. She would run *to* me.

Chloe bolts off the bed and flees to the other side of the room, grabbing a sheet off the floor as she goes, and I sigh.

"So, you want to do it against the wall, then?" I ask in the old language.

She turns her head to the side like a confused puppy.

"I bet you're wishing you'd bothered to learn our language," I say.

CHLOE

Why did I back myself into a corner like this? It's not like being huddled on the bed naked was some vast improvement, but the *heroine huddling in the corner* is as brainless as the *heroine going down that long dark hallway* or the *heroine taking a short cut through the cemetery in the middle of the night.*

My body responds to his proximity... the animal thing inside him. The animal thing inside me. Don't get me wrong, I like Cade a lot—the human, I mean. And I'm very physically attracted. But it isn't this sort of mindless need that I feel when the berserker aims all his erotic energy in my direction.

But it doesn't matter what my body wants. I cannot be mated to a berserker!

Too late.

That one thought repeats over and over in my head like a mantra. But I hear it in the berserker's voice, not my own.

I hold my hands up to ward him away as he stalks closer like a jungle cat sizing up prey. Why don't I have more magic? There are valkyries who have straight up real life undeniable magic. Like they can conjure fire or electricity from their hands and shoot it at people. And yet, here I am, trapped in this cell with a berserker and no handy magic to destroy him with.

My heart lurches and plummets to my stomach at the thought of hurting him. I want to say it's because killing the berserker would kill Cade, too. But I don't want to kill either of them. Everything inside me wants to forget Paris, forget art. Forget all my dreams and just throw my fate in with this guy.

A fucked-up part of me doesn't care about those he killed. He didn't do it from evil. It's the rage. He can't help it. But I could help him control it. Still, I bristle against this as though that would mean my purpose in life is to serve some man. But the way he's looking at me... I might get the better end of this deal. I could keep him sane, and he could keep me in pleasure... a steady drip feed of mind numbing pleasure.

He speaks to me again in the old language and it's a soft growl, somehow inviting even as I know he's barely holding back all his darker instincts. I wonder if that's Cade's influence as well, because it can't really be mine if I'm not touching him. I don't think. I really wish I'd gotten the full valkyrie handbook.

I have no idea what he's saying, and it frustrates me because even though I know he understands me, I still feel like I can't reason with him or have a real discussion. Even so, a secret place inside me loves hearing that language on his tongue.

His eyes glow golden again, and he growls. I feel that growl roll over my body. I feel it penetrate through my skin and into my soul. On the one hand it terrifies me because he is the big bad wolf, and I might be dinner. But I also might be... dinner. And the way he's looking at me, and the evidence of his hard on suggests the delicious possibility of the latter.

His nostrils flare, and I know he can smell me. I can't pretend I don't want him. I can't pretend that every nerve ending in my body isn't lighting up like a Yule tree at the idea of this guy just *claiming me* and damn the consequences.

It's an endless wait while he calculates his next play, and then finally... he moves his chess piece.

Suddenly he's pressing me against the hard stone wall, his hands gripping my wrists, pinning them over my head, that low growl rolling out of him. I whimper and arch toward him as his mouth claims mine. I've never before been kissed in such a savage consuming way. I didn't know kisses like this were real.

It's at once both the most possessive and the most protective touch I've ever received. His growl turns into a purr as he breaks away. He slowly licks over his mark.

"Please... please." It's the only word I can manage. There is this moronic part of me that hates happiness and joy that still wants to fight about this and go through the endless random grocery list of *what if's*, imagining unlikely and impossible scenarios where my fate isn't already entwined with the berserker looming over me, but then the part of me that *isn't* stupid arches her hips up in invitation.

A low pleased growl comes out of the berserker, and he says something to me that I somehow know is completely filthy.

He steps back and pulls me away from the wall, guiding me to the bed. When we get there, he tosses me down on my stomach. He doesn't bother trying to communicate with me in words I can't understand. Instead he positions me as he wants me—on my hands and knees. The wolf wants it doggie style. Of course he does.

I'm shocked when he doesn't just shove his dick inside me. I'm ready for him. I don't need a long sweet prelude. But instead, it's his tongue between my legs. It's as though he needs some part of me to be inside him. I wriggle against his mouth, those slow languid licks driving me crazy, driving me toward the edge.

I moan and whimper, gripping the bed sheets as though they're the only thing that can keep me from careening over the cliff into an abyss I know I'll never recover from.

"Please..." I cry out when he pulls away. Before I can catch my breath, his hard length thrusts inside me. In this moment I feel both unmade and reborn—this new dark creature rising from the ashes with him in this moment as souls and bodies merge together in this ancient act of animal lust.

He speaks to me in the old language, the words are beautiful dark mysteries rolling over me as our bodies dance together and the wave of pleasure builds. Stars die and are born, universes collapse, time stands still as we both reach our peak. And then he bites me, making the mark a real and visible thing that all creatures will see—not just the magical ones.

And now it's done, and there's no going back.

7

CHLOE

The berserker goes over to the food slot and shouts something that sounds like it might be some sort of code. The door opens, and my clothing is tossed inside the cell.

I snatch the clothes and put them on. Now that the moment is passed, now that it's done, there's guilt and shame and second guessing and all these stupid counter-thoughts about why did I just give in to him? Why didn't I fight? I can't be tied to a monster. I can't. I can't. I can't.

"Chloe?"

I look up sharply. I know from the hesitancy in his voice that it's Cade. Oh gods. I'd forgotten about Cade. He just got a live action porno, watching from behind the eyes of the berserker. He saw everything. He *heard* everything. I wonder if he could feel it or if only the berserker was truly fully there for the pleasure.

I look away from his gaze. I can't stand his concern. It only shames me. I'd rather have the monster back than that cloying concern that somehow only makes me feel worse. I brush past him and leave the cell.

No one tries to restrict or stop me. Why would they? It's done.

I'm mated to a berserker and there's no undoing that. There's nowhere I can go far enough that he couldn't find me. There's no way to ever be off his radar again. It would be pointless wearing myself out running from him. And after what we just shared, my traitorous body won't allow me to run from the one who made me feel those things, even if he's more monster than man.

"Chloe!" I hear Cade behind me as I climb the stairs into the main... castle? I'm still not sure how to define this place. But it's very old world, as though we stepped back in time. And at least what I can see on the main floor, there's no technology breaking this illusion.

I run for the front door. The guards, instead of blocking me, hold the door open and step aside, I run out into the darkness, feeling completely disoriented by the night. I run down rolling hills, and then I hear the rip of clothing as I feel something pushing out of my back. I scream at the sudden searing pain of this new thing being born, and then I'm flying. I have large glossy black wings. It feels like I'm swimming in the sky with the stars, floating through wispy clouds.

I feel like I could fly toward the moon and never stop until I broke free of this dimension of reality entirely. Can't I escape the berserker—my mate—now with wings? He doesn't have wings; he can't fly. But I can't fly forever. Already I'm getting tired. I'm unused to the heavy weight of them and all the muscles I've never had nor used before this moment. I'm like a baby learning to crawl.

I let out a strangled, frustrated cry... but it's not a weak human cry. It's a valkyrie shriek, and the sky lights up in response to my voice. I want to fly over the ocean and drop into the cool sea. Could I float on my wings? I laugh out loud as I realize the girl who was afraid of flying has wings now. But it isn't artificial flight, it's the real thing. It's flying I can control.

Until I can't.

I'm out of strength and all at once I start to fall. I panic, but then I stretch my wings out, gliding in for what I'm sure is less than the most graceful landing. I tuck my wings, arms, and legs in to roll as I hit the ground in front of the chateau. I struggle to stand, dusting myself off as my wings disappear somehow inside my body. Well, that's a neat storage trick.

The breeze caresses my back where the fabric of my shirt ripped, and I realize, embarrassed, that the ripping plus the flying has left me without a shirt at all. Fabulous.

I jump as Cade's hand wraps around my arm and he spins me to face him. "Chloe. Are you okay?"

I cover myself, even though I know he's seen it all. I'm not sure if he's asking about my kind-of crash landing or what happened in the cell with the berserker. It hasn't escaped my notice that I've started getting valkyrie powers—more valkyrie powers—since the berserker initiated the mating process the night I met him. First the shriek and lightning. Now the flying and ability to shapeshift. Maybe I'll get fireballs after all.

"Are you okay?" he asks again, concern etching his features.

"The fall wasn't as bad as it looked. I'm pretty aerodynamic now," I say, trying to keep it as light as possible while pretending I'm not standing here on the front lawn without a shirt on. He's got his jeans back on at least.

"I meant what happened before."

"What do *you* think? I know you saw and heard it all... did you *feel* it, too?"

"No." There's a long pause and a deep breath before he says, "But I want to."

This admission somehow shocks me. Cade may be good but he's still a man with normal male desires. His eyes heat with lust as he takes me in. I can't even imagine what I look like standing in only jeans, my hair disheveled from my flight.

The man who couldn't do any of those things with me or to me has had a change of heart. He pulls my arms away from my body, his gaze moving ever so slowly over me. Then, without shifting his gaze from mine, he takes my hand gently in his and presses it against his erection.

I just had sex with this body. I was just completely claimed and possessed by this body. It's unbreakable. And I wanted it. I wanted him even though I knew I shouldn't even though now I am bound forever, my life irrevocably changed.

And I should be angry, at the berserker for marking me and claiming me, at Cade for getting that stupid tattoo without knowing the fucking magic he was playing with. At the fates for toying with my life like this.

I pull away from him and take a few steps back. "I can't."

The reason I can't is that it feels somehow like cheating on my mate. And I hate that I even think that thought, that there is some instinctual loyalty to a man who didn't give me a choice in being his.

Cade's eyes flash golden for a moment. I feel the berserker rising in him. He isn't taking over. I don't even think Cade notices this, but they are both fully here right now. Both fully awake.

Cade takes a step closer to me. "Chloe... I had to watch all of that... hear all of that... I shouldn't have been so noble when I had the chance to take you."

I don't retreat again when he reaches out for me and pulls me into his embrace. He strokes my hair, and then his lips press softly against mine. "Let me have this. Let me feel this with you." He whispers the words against my mouth like a prayer, and I melt against him.

I just had the wild animal version of this with the berserker; can't I have the hearts and flowers romance side with Cade?

In answer to my silent question, he scoops me up in his arms and carries me back inside and up the stairs of the grand entry hall.

"Where are you taking me?"

"There has to be a bedroom in this endless castle."

See? I knew it was a castle! Cade kicks in doors on the second floor like a firefighter looking for kittens to rescue, until he finds a bedroom that meets his approval with a giant four poster king-sized bed and a fireplace.

There's already a fire crackling in it, and I wonder if the staff keeps all the fires lit in the cooler months. The full moon shines in through the window. Cade lays me down on the bed, closes the drapes, and shuts and locks the bedroom door.

I know he's not locking me in. He's locking others out. I think in some twisted place in his mind he thinks he can somehow keep the berserker out even though he's here with us, watching, hearing, but not feeling. I shudder as I wonder what he'll do when he's the one in control again. Will he punish me for this?

Cade strokes my throat over the place where the berserker marked me. Every time his fingertips graze that mark, his eyes turn golden.

"Cade?"

He shakes his head, as if shaking the berserker from his consciousness. "I'm here."

He spends the next hour worshiping me. With his hands. With his tongue. With his cock. Our bodies glide fluidly against each other, soft cries and whimpers from me, groans from him. I feel the monster inside him watching us together, and I can't tell if he's angry or aroused, if he feels betrayed or pleased by the show. Is he a voyeur at heart?

Together we give and receive pleasure until there is nothing else to give or take. And then He's the big spoon and I'm the little spoon as we curl together watching the fire. It takes several minutes for our breath and heartbeats to return to their normal rhythms.

"You aren't the only one here who had your life and plans stolen in an instant," He says quietly.

"I know," I whisper back. But I'd forgotten. I'd been so wrapped up in my own shit and my own need to escape the berserker that I'd forgotten Cade is as permanently tied to him as

I am. And suddenly a very big part of me doesn't want to run, not just because of the way the berserker makes my body feel, but because I don't want to leave Cade alone with a monster who won't be able to control the rage without me. His arm comes over me, his fingers interlacing with mine, and we sleep.

8

CHLOE

The sun bathes the room in light, the fire having long ago died in the grate. I stretch out like a cat and start to wriggle out from under Cade's arm, but his hold tightens on me.

"Somebody was a bad girl last night. I wonder who."

I freeze. Even though I can't twist my body to see his eyes to check, something in his voice and tone sounds different. He's speaking English now, but it's not Cade. It's the berserker.

"Y-you told him you'd share me with him," I say, feeling both panicked and absolutely ridiculous given that it's the *same body*! Even so, they are very different men. They kiss differently. They have sex differently. The berserker moves differently. His voice is different, darker somehow.

He chuckles. "Yes, I gave him permission to take you. I didn't, however, give you permission to be taken."

"Please..." I hate the way my voice cracks. I can't ask him to let me go. We both know that won't happen. It's not even fully possible for it to happen. He can track me until the end of time, and just thinking about that makes me tired before I even try.

He trails kisses over my throat and licks the mark, causing me to shiver, and my core ignites with desire. Unconsciously I open my legs to him.

He chuckles against my throat. "Oh, my little valkyrie, you think we're going to have a nice gentle fuck like you had with the human? Do you believe that will appease me?"

"I... I'm your mate. Y-you can't hurt me." That might sound more convincing if my voice wasn't shaking.

He gently bites my earlobe and growls in my ear, "That depends on your definition of hurt."

The berserker loosens his grip on me, but I don't dare flee. He gets out of bed and stretches, giving me a long, slow show of the perfect body Cade built for him with long hours at the gym.

"Come with me. I doubt you'll want me to chase you down before punishing you. It gets me all worked up."

I want to follow him like a good girl. Really I do. I know how foolish it is to run. And I'm so attracted to him. And I think... he won't hurt me. I'm his mate. Deep down I really really don't think he'll hurt me.

But there is something inside me that just does *not* submit. That's what it means to be a valkyrie. You don't submit. You don't give up. You don't bend to the will of another. You just... don't. It doesn't matter what's right or wrong, rational or irrational, smart or stupid. I simply cannot give in to this man. The berserker doesn't deny or suppress his nature, and neither can I.

I mean yes, I know, last night I kind of gave in to this man, but that's different.

I follow him out of the room. I haven't bothered to shield my nudity even though I know we aren't alone in the house. Some very distinct things have shifted within me, and I find I no longer have the same sense of modesty I had when I arrived. Before the berserker I didn't have any noticeable valkyrie powers, so it was easy to pretend I was human. At some point along the way, that pretending convinced even me, but the truth rips through the illusion as more and more of the valkyrie I've suppressed emerges.

When we get to the main landing I break away and run through the enormous main hall toward the front doors, but guards block my escape. I feel my own rage igniting, heat in my hands, and I glance down to see the fire forming, fire I can and will hurl at them if necessary.

But it isn't necessary.

"Let her go," the berserker commands from behind me.

The guards step aside and open the doors, allowing me to run through to the freedom outside much the same as I did last night. This time the transformation hurts less as my wings unfurl, and flying is just a little bit easier.

In the sunlight I can see my wings aren't solid matte black. They're the iridescent blue-black of a raven. A few of them are green-black and purple-black. So many different colors hidden within the illusion of black.

I fly until I can't go any farther. This time, I manage to coast in for a much more graceful landing at the edge of an open field many miles from the chateau.

There are trees only a few yards from me that lead into a wooded area large enough to get lost in but too small to be called a forest.

I wonder how much time I've bought myself, how far away the berserker is, and how easily he can track me. And then what happens? I don't know what to do next. I know the absolute futility of this. But I feel more and more out-of-control of myself these days.

There is something distinctly animal inside me—as if sprouting wings and flying through the sky doesn't make that crystal clear all on its own.

Before I can decide what to do, the berserker steps out from behind the trees. He carries rope and something else which I can't determine at this distance. His eyes glow golden.

"Well, I read *that* room wrong. I guess you *do* want to get me all worked up chasing you."

My heart thunders in my chest. I can't fly anymore, but still I won't just give in. I won't beg him. I'm his fucking mate. If he hurts me there will be nothing that can save him. I have fire now. And I will use it if I have to.

As if to illustrate this point, I allow the ball of fire to form fully in my hand in front of me. I stare at it, still barely believing I can do this now. Then I stare at the berserker.

He chuckles. "There she is. There's my girl."

I want to say I'm not his girl. He barely even knows me. But the berserker knows the me I've hidden even from myself.

He takes off, running at blurring speed toward me, so fast, I startle. The fire dies in my hand, and in my panic I can't get it to re-ignite, so I turn and run. It takes less than a minute for him to run me down like some hapless gazelle.

I struggle and fight against him. He growls. His body covers mine. We're both naked. I think he's going to just take me out here in the middle of this field, but instead he grabs my hand and places it over his tattoo. He takes a couple of long slow breaths and then pushes me away. Can't let Cade fully out, after all.

"I thought you wanted to play," he says, looking almost hurt. "Why open your legs to me if you're going to make me chase you?"

It's so weird hearing him in English. I really didn't think he had such faculty with language... any language. And I didn't expect him to be so... sarcastic. I mean, he *is* rage after all. Snarky wit didn't seem like it would make it into that package.

I shrug, but he's not having it. He stands, then picks me up and carries me back over to the trees. I haven't so much given in as decided I don't want to waste any more energy running or flying from him right now. I convince myself I'll find a way to escape him another day... wait until his guard is down. Or maybe I'll be able to use the fire some day. I always have it as a backup. I *can* fight him if I need to.

My heart isn't in any of these plans, however, and my body definitely isn't. The closeness of his skin against mine... the way I can feel his heartbeat as he carries me across the field... the determined sense of purpose in his gait... it all... does things to me. I don't know exactly what will happen when we get to the trees, but I have a pretty good idea.

He sets me on my feet next to one of the large oaks. "Stay," he says as if I'm some disobedient house pet.

I'm about to protest but he growls, and so I stand there. I'm not giving in. I'm just taking a break from fighting and running. That's all this is. Like a coffee break. I mean for fuck's sake, he can't just drag me off to his cave like some barbarian and think I'm going to be the good little woman without a single complaint.

He goes back to the field and picks up the things he dropped. I swallow hard when he approaches with the ropes and the other things in the bundle I still can't determine through the maze of all the rope.

"What's that for?"

He gives me a look as though he thinks I'm very very stupid. "You were a bad girl."

My mouth drops open, and I just gape at him—probably reinforcing his earlier assessment of me.

"Pull your wings in and face the tree."

"I... but... I..."

"Now," he growls.

You would think it's my mask of humanity that causes me to follow his command, but it isn't. It would be so easy if that were the truth. No, there's a fire lit inside me, a growing arousal between my legs. What he wants to do next? I don't know his exact plan, but it excites me.

"I could kill you with fire," I say.

He chuckles. "You could try."

The fact that I know even with fire and wings he might still be able to win, stirs something primal within me... as though a bright neon sign flashes over his head. This imaginary sign communicates one word: *Worthy.*

I don't know why that's the word I associate with him. But it is. And I realize with sudden striking clarity that a human male was never going to be enough for me.

I turn slowly away from him and pull in my wings as he requested.

He's behind me a moment later, his hot breath in my ear, his hands roaming over me, groping, fondling... marking his territory.

"Cade is watching", he whispers. "He's getting a front row seat to the real you. I want you to be loud for him."

He picks something up from the ground... a piece of black fabric which he ties over my eyes.

Then he takes my arms and lowers them, holding them out in front of me while he binds them together with rope much softer than I expected it to be. When he's finished, he raises my arms over my head and binds me to the tree. He ties me at the waist as well but leaves my legs free.

He's silent and I'm silent. And then the whip begins to fall across my back. I'm not even sure if he's actually punishing me for sleeping with Cade or if this is just a game we're playing. I can't tell. It feels real, but it doesn't feel unsafe which I don't understand.

He doesn't give me a safe word. I don't ask for one. The link between us goes so much deeper than the need for verbal communication. I knew that last night when he claimed me.

Aren't berserkers crazy and unstable? I'm supposed to run if I see one. I never thought to question this wisdom. And now I've foolishly allowed one to tie me to a tree to act out his Fifty Shades fantasies. Though this feels so much more real than some billion-aire with a whips and chains fetish.

All at once I'm crying. It starts off as polite and proper tears sliding down my face... you know... pretty crying. The kind in a slow camera zoom of a melancholy period film. Restrained tears.

But within a few minutes these polite tears have turned to sobs, and yet I don't beg him because I'm not sure I want him to stop. There are so many things that have been locked inside and held close while I was pretending to be a human.

I'm pretty sure he's broken skin. But I know with all my other magic, I'll heal quickly. The whip stops and his tongue trails across the lashes. He growls as he does this, and a shiver runs down my spine. I wonder if he's crossing into a place that's dangerous for me, all while my hands are bound and I can't calm him. But the taste of me seems to calm him, yet that feeling that the big bad wolf just might eat me, comes over me again.

Before I can let the panic set in, his hand moves between my legs and he speaks low in my ear. "When I'm away, you can have sweet comforting sex and cuddles with the human. Then I'm going to punish you for it. I will use everything in that box on you and more. And when I'm finished, I will fuck you in a way so that you know and never forget which one of us you truly belong to."

Moments later, I hear a buzzing sound, and then the source of that buzz is pressing hard against my clit.

"Don't come," he growls in my ear, even as my moans and twisting and squirming grow more intense.

I don't know if I'm trying to get more contact or less. I can't decide if the vibrations are too strong or not strong enough. And I don't think I can follow the direction not to come because it's not entirely in my control.

I've reached the top of the roller coaster, about to free fall when the buzzing stops.

"Please…"

It's spoken softly but I know he heard it. He has ears that hear the quietest of sounds. It's the first time I've begged him for anything today, and that softly spoken word feels like I lost whatever maybe-game we were playing.

Something sharp and pointed strokes gently against my cheek, and I shudder as I realize it's a claw.

"I could slice you open. Do you know why I don't?" His voice is still a low growl, calm words spoken against my ear. Secrets.

"N-no."

"Because you're *mine*. It's a very fortunate position to be in. Bad things happen to those who aren't mine."

He just *had* to remind me of what he is. What he's done. I haven't seen the bodies, but I know they exist. All the people he's killed with no remorse. And yet, here I am, melting against him, whimpering like a porn star. And even though my mouth isn't begging him to take me, my body is. And I can't even say she's wrong to want him.

His effect is visceral.

I hear that claw slice through the air a moment before the ropes around me are sliced apart. They fall to the ground like shredded paper, and he spins me, pressing my back against the trunk of the tree. He rips the blindfold off and I'm staring into hungry feral yellow eyes, and in this moment I am truly scared because I can see the animal edging out the more civilized side of him... it's the part of him that knows no language and can't be reasoned with.

"Cade?" I know he's the berserker, and Cade isn't coming out right now, but I don't know what else to call him.

He only growls as his gaze pans hungrily over me.

"Do you know who I am?" I ask, fearing he's really lost the part of himself that knows I'm his... the thing that was supposed to protect me.

That rumbling growl comes again, fangs visible. Claws out. I'm pinned, trapped by his huge body against this tree, and he's lost all sense. And even though the ropes no longer hold me, he holds me, and I can't wriggle my hand free to calm him.

He sniffs me, a long slow inhale at my neck. Then he licks over his mark and purrs, and then he's fucking me senseless against the tree. He's lost language, but I don't care. I don't need his permission to come. I just do it. My shriek when I do come isn't rage, but it still sends jagged sparks of lightning across the sky. He growls again as he spills inside me. Then as our bodies are still joined, those feral golden eyes stare at me.

They stare at me for a long time. I'm breathing hard. He's breathing hard. And we're just looking at each other. Finally, he lets go of me. My shaking hand rises to press against his chest. He doesn't stop me. He doesn't say a word even when I know he's regained the ability to speak. He holds my hand against his chest until his eyes turn back to that pure crystal blue, and I know I'm looking at Cade.

Cade looks horrified, disgusted by what just happened. I know he doesn't intend it this way, but his horror shames me, as though I'm the victim of an abuser. But the berserker isn't an abuser. He's an animal. He's rage. And I'm the only breathing soul safe from him.

"He could have killed you. He wanted to."

I shake my head. "The mark protected me. Even his darkest side knows not to hurt me."

"Knows not to hurt you? Are you fucking kidding me right now, Chloe? He whipped you until you bled, and you just took it. And I couldn't do anything to stop him. I tried to come out and save you."

Has it not occurred to him that I don't need saving?

I don't want to have this argument with him. I know what it must look like, especially when he doesn't share the mating bond and he doesn't feel the things the berserker feels or the things I feel, and he lacks the connection for that free flow of information. I know how it looks. But I also know what it is even if I have no words to explain with.

I pull him to me and kiss him, mainly to shut him up and distract him from trying to protect me from the things his body does to me when Cade's not in charge of it.

Cade is swayed easily to my new plan, and then the soft romantic sweet sex happens, and we curl up together in the soft grass for a much deserved nap.

9

CHLOE

Weeks go by where I find myself passed between the berserker and Cade. It's like having a threesome relationship with Superman and Clark Kent. With the berserker it's all animal lust and darkness and punishments that I somehow want... punishments for all the romance with Cade. Yes, I know how twisted this is. Part of me thinks the berserker is jealous of the softer feelings I have toward Cade, and that he knows I withhold those things from him even though he's my real mate, not the human.

I've learned that the chateau belonged to another berserker, but that berserker owns several other estates, and it has been agreed by the collective that it's right to give it to us. I'm still trying to process that I'm basically living in a castle. In the past several weeks I've learned Cade, the human, has his own wealth—some kind of internet marketing business that requires very little actual work on his part now that it's all up and running. So between that and the berserker's hivemind inheritance, money is one thing I'll never have to worry about again.

I lie in bed facing the berserker. He's doing something between a growl and a purr—like he can't decide which to settle on. My hand trembles as I reach out and place it on the tattoo that gave birth to him. I'm surprised when he allows this. He hasn't let Cade fully out in several days, and I miss him desperately as one might miss civilization after a long time out in the wilderness. I keep waiting for the berserker to push me away, to decide he's calm enough and my services are no longer needed, but his hand is on top of mine, pressing my palm to his chest, holding it there, just breathing in the peace.

I feel his heart rate calm to that of a normal human. I watch his eyes melt back to blue as the calmness smooths out the stress lines on his face.

"Cade?"

He looks at me, but something's not right. I can feel it. It isn't the same as the normal feeling of being watched by the berserker from deep inside the human. No, this feeling of surveillance rests more on the surface.

"Cade?" My voice is more panicked this time, and I'm willing myself not to cry as a terrifying suspicion takes hold in my mind.

"Cade!" I shout his name as though I can claw my way through the berserker's soul and pull Cade out from the twisted wreckage and save him.

"You killed him!"

I realize now that the berserker is like a virus that kills the host but somehow lives on, animating the shell like a zombie. I'm beating at his chest now, screaming, and crying. Not the valkyrie shriek, no, it's those stupid pathetic human tears—the shriek that makes me feel weak instead of powerful, the one that darkens my world instead of lighting up the sky in the jagged lines of my fury.

"Stop it," he says. He's finally had enough and grips my wrists in his. "Stop. It. I didn't kill him. We merged. It's finally complete. I gave him immortality. He's now part of the berserker collective, so much more powerful than he ever could have been as a fragile human."

"You *killed* him!" I shout again. And it really has less impact when I'm not beating my tiny fists against his chest. I don't even have the concentration to make fire right now.

"I am the berserker, and I am Cade. No experience or memory is lost on either side. No personality trait is lost. It's all in here."

"Then why don't I feel him!"

The berserker bends down, and I shudder as his tongue moves across his mark. I don't want to admit it's not just the magic of the mark that makes me feel what I do with him. I don't like to admit that it's more than carnal lust.

"Because you don't want to see it," he growls.

He pulls back and he's angry, but it's not the anger of berserker fury. It's a very human kind of anger, the kind we ascribe all sorts of meaning and value to.

"You can't accept darkness in Cade. So if you see something dark, it can't be Cade, it can only be the berserker. And you can't see warmth in the berserker. Well, Chloe, you're going to have to pick one. Either the berserker can feel something more than fury and animal lust, or Cade is still in here."

He pulls me into his embrace and gives me one of those sweeping movie sort of kisses with the background music and the rolling panoramic landscapes. One of those kisses where two heartbeats blend into one coordinated rhythm as if on a mission together to save the world. And it doesn't feel like the berserker in this moment.

But when he finally pulls away from me, he's breathing hard and his eyes are golden.

"You're going to have to accept both the light and the dark. You can't run from me to Cade anymore. I am Cade now. We can't un-merge. It's done."

"I didn't even get to say goodbye."

"I didn't go anywhere, Chloe! Stop mourning me!" He grips my shoulders and forces me to look into his eyes.

And that's when I see it... see him, the merging of the monster and the man, and nothing will ever be the same again, because I have no more excuses not to let myself love him. I can't say I'm imprisoned... that he wouldn't do anything in his power to make me happy, because deep down I know that's not true. He told me a few days ago that I could go to art school, that he wouldn't stop my dreams.

I can't say I fear him because he may be the big scary, but he's my big scary. His ruthless ferocity isn't aimed in my direction but in the direction of anything or anyone that might seek to harm me.

He trails his finger over my mark, and I shudder under that touch.

"Cade?"

"That's what I'm calling myself now."

I ignore the sarcasm and just say, "Okay."

"Okay, what?"

"Okay to everything. Just... okay."

And I finally accept my fate and give him the very last piece of me, my heart.

I HOPE YOU ENJOYED BERSERKER. It was just a small taste into this bigger world I'm building. If you liked this, be sure to check out my latest release: VALKYRIE, it's the love story of Odin and Freyja and Cade makes a cameo appearance. If you turn the page, you'll find a teaser scene from when Odin meets Freyja.

THANK you so much for reading!

Kitty ^.^

TEASER SCENE FROM VALKYRIE: CHAPTER THREE:

WHEN ODIN MEETS FREYJA (ODIN POV)

N ot all that long ago in the grand scheme of things...

AN OLD WOMAN sits alone at a table away from the live music, a mug of hot liquid in her frail hands. Her head raises abruptly, and her gaze narrows on mine. Then one shriveled finger beckons me nearer.

I turn to look behind me, even though I know she means me. I consider just walking out. There's something deeply unnerving about her, but against all my better judgment, I cross the room and sit in the chair she indicates.

"I know what's coming for you," she says cryptically. Leaning in she asks, "Do you want to know your fate?"

I just chuckle. "I don't believe in fate. And I have no gold on me to pay you, witch."

I start to get up, but she grips my wrist hard. "Sit. Down." She closes her eyes for a moment as though waiting for information to be dropped into her mind, as though in a trance.

Finally, her eyes open and level on me—an eerie light blue. "Odin."

Goosebumps prickle out over my arm under the heat of her hand at hearing my name on her lips.

Okay, I'm impressed. It's not that no one knows who I am, but I wear many guises and can easily fade into any crowd.

"You like power," she observes. "Power and knowledge. You can never get enough of it. You think knowledge is power, but sometimes it's just the opposite."

"Doesn't everyone want power? Why even live if you only exist to serve the whims or values of others? Most creatures are slaves, and I've made great sacrifices to get to where I am."

"Indeed, you have."

Her gaze rakes over me. No matter what form I take, I can't ever hide the lack of one eye or the scar around my throat from the rope that finally snapped after nine days hanging from a tree. I survived that, and in the end, the runes spilled all their secrets to me. What could ever possibly take me out after that?

I can't imagine the arrogance of a fate that would think to come for me.

As if in answer to my internal question she says, "The wolves are very angry with you, Odin."

This announcement jars me, but I school my features, revealing nothing. It's just an old woman peering into a cup. What does she know?

The witch continues, "You will lose all your power to a giant wolf, a wolf larger than even the greatest dragon in all the realms. He is the keeper of all the memories of the wolves. And he knows, Odin. He knows what you did. His name is Fenrir. The great wolf spirit searches for you even now. Someday he will find what he seeks. In that time there will come a great battle. To you, it will seem to be the end of the world. And you're right... it *is* the end of the world... for you. Let's give it a name, shall we? All epic fights must have their own name."

She looks into her cup, and I wonder if she's reading tea leaves. I'd thought her to be drinking something stronger, but perhaps not. Every part of me wants to get up and flee this tavern, but I feel compelled to stay and wait and hear the rest of my supposed fate.

Finally she looks up and smiles. "I've got it... Ragnarok. It's got a nice doom ring to it, don't you think?"

"I never go into fights I can't win," I say. And it's true. Every battle is won before I ever set foot on the battlefield. Every move and countermove laid out. By the time I go into a fight, I know exactly what my enemy will do. They're always so transparent, their wills and desires, their hopes and fears all laid out before me, like vulnerable infants left in the woods to the wolves.

And I am that wolf.

"You'll go into this one... and you'll know you'll lose."

"Why would I ever do such a thing? It doesn't sound anything like me."

She shrugs. "The norns don't exist at my beck and call. They tell me what they will, and the cup has now gone dark. I have nothing more to give you."

"You're wrong, witch. I never lose. I won't lose. And I won't die. Mark my words, I will stand the victor at the end of this supposed Ragnarok."

"It's fate. An unbreakable prophesy. It can't be changed. I would get my affairs in order if I were you."

"As I said, I don't believe in fate."

She rises from the table and levels a hard gaze at me for several seconds as though she's not sure if she wants to tell me something. Finally, she decides.

"I once knew another king who tried to thwart his death. I was the fate that ended him. And he even had a provision to escape it, which you do not. Count yourself lucky that you don't have such false hope. Now he's only a bad memory. You'll fare no better."

With that pronouncement, she brushes past me to leave.

"Freyja," I say, my voice soft.

I think she didn't hear me, but the tension in her shoulders suggests otherwise. She stops. She heard me. She turns back to face me, the glamour falling off her like sheets of water to reveal her true form.

There's a sharp intake of breath, and I realize it's mine. I'd heard of her legendary beauty, but nothing could prepare me to encounter it face-to-face.

Painted over her exquisite loveliness is an expression of wariness. Is someone after her? Who would dare harm the fair Queen of the Vanir? And a volva of so much power? I felt her power at a distance well before I saw her crone form—the mask she draws up to conceal her beauty from the world.

Who else could it be but her?

I'm standing here, staring at her like an idiot, fantasizing about the better things we could be doing right now than discussing my untimely future fated death. Finally, I break the silence.

"Even more beautiful than the skalds suggest." I can't decide if I want to ask her on a date or to help me fight this. Maybe we could discuss battle strategy over dinner.

She rolls her eyes. "How did you know it was me?"

In truth, I didn't at first. This is the first time we've met in person, but she is known. And even her glamour can't hide who she is for long.

I point to my eye patch. "I gave up a lot to see and know a lot. You'd be shocked by all I've learned from inside the well."

"And yet... you couldn't see the prophecy of your own demise. I'd get a refund."

I wink at her, but that move never really comes off right. "Well, I do have the blind spot on this one side, you know."

"Cute."

But I have her. She smirked a little. She turns to leave, clearly done before the banter has even started.

I grab her arm, and she bristles. My hand immediately falls away. I'm not foolish enough to test a volva's patience—certainly not one as powerful as this. "Freyja, help me. I know you have the power to save me."

"I'm not in the business of fighting pointless battles with fate. Get your affairs in order and forget about it. Live your life while you have it. Goodnight, Odin."

With this final pronouncement, she leaves the tavern. She may have decided that was the end of the discussion, but our conversation has only just begun.

VALKYRIE IS available at all major online retailers in ebook and available at some retailers in both paperback and hardcover.

Made in the USA
Columbia, SC
22 March 2023

13910989R00062